Charles William Heaton

The Threshold of Chemistry

SALZWASSER
VERLAG

Charles William Heaton

The Threshold of Chemistry

Reprint of the original, first published in 1861.

1st Edition 2022 | ISBN: 978-3-37506-775-5

Verlag (Publisher): Salzwasser Verlag GmbH, Zeilweg 44, 60439 Frankfurt, Deutschland
Vertretungsberechtigt (Authorized to represent): E. Roepke, Zeilweg 44, 60439 Frankfurt, Deutschland
Druck (Print): Books on Demand GmbH, In de Tarpen 42, 22848 Norderstedt, Deutschland

THE THRESHOLD OF CHEMISTRY.

THE

THRESHOLD OF CHEMISTRY:

AN EXPERIMENTAL INTRODUCTION TO THE SCIENCE.

BY

CHARLES WILLIAM HEATON, F.C.S.,

DEMONSTRATOR OF PRACTICAL CHEMISTRY TO CHARING-CROSS HOSPITAL.

With Numerous Illustrations.

LONDON:
CHAPMAN AND HALL, 193 PICCADILLY.
1861.

PREFACE.

Most persons of experience in the subject of education, agree that the natural bent of a very large number of boys lies towards the physical sciences. If no circumstances occur to call forth this bent, the boy's pursuits fall into other channels, and, it may be, he succeeds well in those channels. Still, the path which he walks in the world will not be altogether that of Nature's choosing. He will always remain, more or less, to use Bentham's celebrated simile, "the round peg stuck into the three-cornered hole," and it is against this unnatural constriction of the mental shape, that the modern science of education appears to be chiefly striving.

The chief object of the following pages is to furnish, as it were, a *test-book* for the detection and nourishment of such boyish tastes as may lie towards chemistry.

I believe there is nothing in the book but what a boy of ordinary capacity may readily understand without the aid of a master; and I am sure that there is no experiment given in it which may not be performed easily and safely (with moderate care) by a boy. The instructions are so minute, that I believe a misunderstanding to be almost impossible.

I have taken great pains to render the pursuit of the science as inexpensive as possible, and, as far as I know, no book which has yet appeared has assisted the student to so many experiments at so slight a cost.

I sincerely hope that it may supply a want which, as a boy-student, I felt very strongly.

Although I address myself mainly to boys, I believe that any person who wishes to acquire for himself a knowledge of the leading facts and principles of the science, will find the book of use to him.

C. W. H.

Charing-Cross Hospital, 1861.

CONTENTS.

CHAPTER I.

INTRODUCTION.

	PAGE
Expense of Chemical Experiments ...	3
Bottles and Apparatus ...	5

CHAPTER II.

ELEMENTS.

Four Elements of Aristotle ...	10
Chemical Elements ...	11
Metallic and Non-Metallic Elements ...	14
List of Elements ...	15

CHAPTER III.

CHEMICAL AFFINITY.

Difference Between Mixture and Combination ...	16
Chemical Affinity ...	18
Double Decomposition ...	21
Acids, Bases, and Salts ...	22

CHAPTER IV.

OXYGEN.

Preparation ...	25
Pneumatic Trough—Method of Working with Gases ...	28
Properties ...	33
Nature of Combustion ...	41
Respiration ...	42
Other Properties of Oxygen ...	43
Ozone ...	44

CHAPTER V.

HYDROGEN.

PAG

Preparation 46
Collecting Gases by Displacement 49
Balloons 50
WATER 53
Experiments on Water 54
COMBINING PROPORTIONS 62
1st *Law.—Law of Constant Proportion* 63
2nd *Law.—Law of Equivalent Proportion* 64
3rd *Law.—Law of Multiple Proportion* 65
4th *Law.—Law of Compound Proportion* 66
Symbols 66
Properties of Water 68
Crystallization 69
Impurities of Water 70
Distillation 70
Filtration 72
Binoxide of Hydrogen 73

CHAPTER VI.

NITROGEN.

Preparation 74
THE AIR 75
Oxides of Nitrogen 77
Protoxide of Nitrogen 78
Nitric Acid 79
Oxy-Acids, or Oxygen Acids.—Oxy-Salts 83
Ammonia 86

CHAPTER VII.

CHLORINE.—IODINE.—BROMINE.—FLUORINE.

Chlorine 89
Preparation 89
Oxides of Chlorine 92
Chloric Acid.—Chlorate of Potash 92
Hydrochloric Acid 94

PAGE
Hydracids, or Hydrogen Acids.—Haloid Salts 95
Iodine 97
Bromine 98
Fluorine 98
Hydrofluoric Acid 99

CHAPTER VIII.

SULPHUR.—PHOSPHORUS.—SELENIUM.

Sulphur 100
Oxides of Sulphur 101
Sulphurous Acid 101
Sulphuric Acid 102
Hydrosulphuric Acid 103
Phosphorus 106
Amorphous Phosphorus 110
Phosphoric Acid 111
Hydrates of Phosphoric Acid 111
Phosphoretted Hydrogen 113
Selenium 114

CHAPTER IX.

CARBON.—BORON.—SILICON.

Carbon 115
Oxides of Carbon 116
Carbonic Oxide 116
Carbonic Acid 118
Coal-Gas 120
Nature of Flame.—Blowpipe 123
Davy Lamp 127
Bisulphide of Carbon 129
Boron 130
Silicon 130
Silicic Acid 130

CHAPTER X.

THE METALS.

	PAGE
General Physical Characteristics	132
METALLIC COMBINATIONS	133
Constitution of Oxy-Salts	135
Meaning of Neutrality	135
Polybasic Acids	136
Law of Neutrality	137
Acid Salts	138
Basic Salts	138
Classification of Metals	138
CLASS I.—*Metals of the Alkalies and Earths*	139
Potassium	139
Potash	141
Coloured Flames	143
Salts of Potash	145
Other Compounds of Potassium	145
Sodium—Soda	145
Barium—Baryta	147
Strontium—Strontia	148
Calcium—Lime	148
Magnesium—Magnesia	150
Aluminum—Alumina	151

CHAPTER XI.

METALS—*continued.*

CLASS II.—*Metals Proper, Fusible Below a Red Heat*...	153
Lead	153
Manipulation with Beakers, &c.	155
Tin...	159
Arsenic	162
Marsh's Test for Arsenic	163
Antimony	165
Bismuth	166
Zinc	167
Mercury	168

PAGE

CLASS III.—*Metals Proper, Infusible Below a Red Heat*

Iron 172
Manganese 176
Chromium 179
Cobalt 180
Nickel 182
Copper 182
Tungsten 185
Silver 186
Platinum 187
Gold 190

THE

THRESHOLD OF CHEMISTRY.

CHAPTER I.

INTRODUCTION.

I REMEMBER when I was a boy I used sometimes to find it rather difficult to amuse myself during the Wednesday and Saturday half-holidays.

Sometimes, indeed, I could play at cricket, or top, or marbles, and then it was all very well; but sometimes it rained, and I could not go out, or else I could not find any one to play with if I did; and then it was that, as I had no brothers, I was driven to my own resources for amusement. Like most other boys, I soon got tired of reading, and began to long for something which should employ my fingers as well as my head.

At last, very fortunately for me as I now think, a boy a little older than myself, with whom I had become acquainted, took me to his house, and showed me how he amused himself during his spare time. He took me into a little room—a room, indeed, scarcely larger than a cupboard—the walls of which were entirely covered with shelves, and the shelves with a confused medley of bottles, flasks, lamps, and glass tubes, which struck me as having a wonderfully knowing look: and when he unfolded a few of his marvels, and showed me how one colourless liquid may mingle with another colourless liquid, and produce a blue, or red, or yellow colour; or how a little piece of common brimstone rubbed in a mortar with a shining white crystal, gives a flash of light and a loud explosion, I was completely captivated by this new subject of chemistry, and went home, resolved to try what I could do for myself—whether I could not learn to do some of these wonderful things too, and understand the reason of them.

From that time I was a chemist. I spent all my pocket money (which was little enough) in buying chemicals and apparatus, and I soon found that the science which I was slowly learning was one of the most interesting in the world; for I began to understand that there is scarcely anything which takes place in the world around us but what is in some way or other connected with chemistry. If I saw a candle burning, I recollected that the materials of which it was made were not being destroyed, as I had previously imagined, but were only changing their shape, and being converted into invisible gases, which were passing off into the air of the room. Or if I lit a lucifer match, I understood that the reason it caught fire was, that the curious substance called phosphorus which it contained, combined so eagerly with the oxygen, which forms part of the air, that it gave out light and heat in doing so.

In like manner, many other things which before

were utterly meaningless and incomprehensible to me, now began to be clear and interesting.

From that time to the present my interest and love for chemistry have never flagged, but have daily grown stronger as the amount of my knowledge has increased; and the performance of any new chemical experiment affords me almost, if not quite, as much pleasure now as it would have done when I was a boy.

I recommend the study of chemistry to every boy who has the opportunity of pursuing it. If he will but work honestly at it, not solely with the wish to amuse himself, but also with a true desire to learn its facts, he will not fail to find it, as I have done, a most entertaining and profitable pursuit.

To any boy who wishes to learn to perform chemical experiments, I have just two pieces of advice to give :—

1. Work patiently.
2. Work neatly.

Expense of Chemical Experiments.—In order to acquire a practical knowledge of chemistry, the only kind of knowledge which is of much use, it is necessary that you should make a great many experiments. This necessity is of course greatly diminished if you are fortunate enough to be able to attend lectures; but the knowledge derived from the actual performance of the processes described, is so much more solid, and so much more easily remembered, that in any case it is greatly to be preferred to that obtained solely from books or lectures, however valuable they may be.

The sole difficulty standing in the way of an experimental knowledge of chemistry, is its real or supposed expense. But this difficulty will be found to be more one of appearance than of reality. Of course I do not mean to say that it may not be made an expensive study. On the contrary, it is not an uncommon thing for a thousand pounds to be expended in fitting up a chemical laboratory; and in any case advanced students will have to go to a considerable expense. What I mean is, that a very extensive and highly valuable knowledge of the science may be acquired at an extremely small cost; and I strongly advise the young student to be as economical as he possibly can in this respect, for the habit of working with simple means, and of substituting cheap and self-constructed contrivances for expensive apparatus, is one which will facilitate his progress in the science to a most amazing degree.

Of course many things must be bought; but chemicals and chemical apparatus are so very cheap in the present day, that if everything necessary for the performance of the experiments in this book were bought ready prepared (which, with contrivance, is quite superfluous), the expense would be very trifling.

What materials you must buy may be procured of almost all operative chemists. I buy most of my things of Messrs. Jackson and Townson, of 89 Bishopsgate Street, London, and from my own experience, and that of many of my friends, I can strongly recommend them. Their things are always cheap and good.

Bottles.—A great many of the materials described in the following pages must be kept in bottles. Some few of them, such as the acids, ether, bisulphide of carbon, potassium, and the like, require stoppered bottles, though it is possible in some cases to manage with corks soaked in melted white wax. The great majority of the substances, however, may be preserved in common corked bottles, or even in pill-boxes: you must use your discretion in this. Of course, *deliquescent* solids, or such as absorb moisture from the air, must be kept tightly corked or stoppered.

Lamps.—For nearly all purposes the common spirit-lamp, with wood-naphtha for fuel, is sufficient. The lamp may be had for a shilling or eighteenpence. The naphtha costs one shilling a pint.

If you are so fortunate as to be able to employ gas, it is greatly to be preferred to all other sources of heat, both on account of its cheapness and convenience. It may be conveyed through a vulcanized india-rubber tube to an argand burner with a copper chimney (*a*, fig. 1).

Fig. 1.

A make-shift spirit-lamp may be constructed by passing a piece of glass tube, one inch long, through a cork fitting into a small bottle. A little piece of tube, closed at one end, may be used as a cap for it. The wick is made of common lamp cotton (fig. 1, *b*).

Supports.—The most generally useful kind of support is the *retort stand.* This is an iron rod, fixed in a solid stand, and with rings of various sizes, which can be fastened to it with a screw at any height and in any position required (fig. 2, *a*).

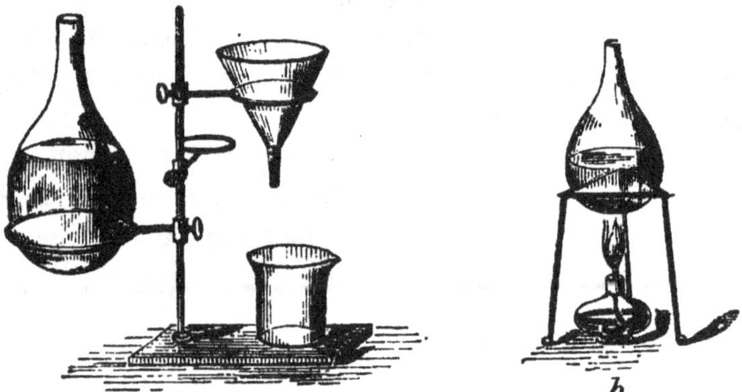

a b

Fig. 2.

Substitutes for these retort stands, which answer extremely well, can be made by twisting stout iron wire into triangular tripods, like that shown at *b*.

Flasks, Test-tubes, &c.—No piece of apparatus is more generally useful in chemistry than the common Florence oil-flask.

They must be cleansed from oil by means of sulphuric acid, or a strong solution of potash, and for some experiments they require to be dried inside. This would at first sight appear to be a matter of difficulty, but it is very easy when you know how to set about it. The same process applies to many other forms of apparatus.

Wash the flask perfectly clean, rinsing it out the last time with a little distilled water. Then, after allowing it to drain for a minute or two, warm it gently, by moving it about over the flame of a lamp. This will convert a portion of the water inside it into vapour, and this vapour may now be expelled by putting one end of a long glass tube to the bottom of it, and drawing a current of air through it with the mouth, by sucking at the other end of the tube. If this be repeated a few times, the flask will be dry.

Test-tubes are incessantly wanted. They are short pieces of glass tube closed at one end, and are made of all sizes. The most useful size for ordinary purposes is about five inches long by three quarters of an inch wide.

A dozen of these, with a large one for oxygen (page 28), will be quite sufficient.

When you wish to heat anything in one of them,

Fig. 3.

it is convenient to twist a piece of soft copper wire round it, with one end projecting to serve for a handle. This prevents the hot tube from burning your fingers.

Beakers are of very great use. They are made of two different shapes, one of which (*a*, fig. 4) has a lip. This is the one which I prefer for most purposes. The other is rather taller, and has no lip. They are sold in nests, and should never be heated except on a sand-bath (page 80).

Fig. 4.

Basins and Crucibles.—A few Berlin-ware basins of different sizes are essential. At page 155 you will find a description of the way in which liquids are poured from them; *a* and *b*, in fig. 5, show two of the most useful shapes: *c* represents a little porcelain crucible with a cover. These are very useful, as they stand a high temperature when used with care.

Fig. 5.

Distilled Water.—In all delicate experiments, such as when solutions are to be made, or tests applied, distilled water must be used. Common water contains many impurities which quite unfit it for these purposes. Distilled water costs about sixpence a gallon. If you are unable to procure it, you must be content with rain-water, which is next to it in purity.

All other necessary details of apparatus will be found in the order that they occur.

CHAPTER II.

ELEMENTS.

Four Elements of Aristotle.—EVERY one knows the old saying, "There are four elements,—earth, air, fire, and water." It was first pronounced by the celebrated Greek philosopher, Aristotle, who lived more than 2000 years ago; and it contains a concise summary of his opinions about the nature and composition of this beautiful world in which we live. The earth, according to him, contained nothing but these four things, and these, by their union together, produced all the wonderful and varied forms of nature. Of course he supposed that each of them was simple in its nature—that it was not possible to divide any one of them into two or more simpler forms; and this is the reason that they have obtained the name of elements, they being, according to him, the materials, as it were, of which the world is built up.

Now although this theory of Aristotle's was believed for so long a time, and although even now we repeat his words so frequently, yet unfortunately they are not true. He began in this instance at the wrong end of his subject; and instead of endeavouring to ascertain what the facts really were, and *then* attempting to account for them, he made a number of speculations on the causes of things, which were little better than guesses, and many of which have accordingly turned out to be quite at variance with the truth. It was very much as if a man were to attempt to construct a house by building from the roof downwards.

The modern science of chemistry has completely upset Aristotle's theory, by showing that out of his four so-called elements, three,—namely, earth, air, and water, are either compounds, or mixtures of other bodies, while fire is not a substance at all, but only an *effect.*

Chemical Elements. — Chemists have given the name of element to a number of substances—about sixty in all—which they, with all their skill and endeavours, are unable to *decompose*, that is, to divide, or separate into other bodies. It does not by any means follow that these elements are really elementary, or simple in their nature. Probably many of them will, some day or other, be proved to be compounds, and then they must be removed from the list of elements. All that chemists mean to assert is, that they are at present unable to decompose these substances.

This world, and everything which it contains, the plants and animals which live and grow upon it, from the smallest weed to the forest tree, and from the most minute insect to the gigantic elephant,—the air we breathe, the water we drink, and the stones upon which we tread—are all formed by the union together in various proportions of these few elements.

Now it requires the greatest care in judging whether any substance is elementary or compound in its nature. The mere appearance is no guide whatever, for very many substances which appear perfectly simple, and which, without experiment, we should never suspect of containing other things, are in reality compounds.

Sugar, for example. You would certainly never imagine that a pure, white lump of sugar could contain anything at all resembling charcoal; and yet so it is. Try the experiment for yourself, and you will soon be convinced of it.

Take a small glass *beaker*, one about four inches high will do very well, put it on a plate or a board, in case it should crack during the experiment; then put into it one or two lumps of sugar, and pour a few drops of hot water on the sugar.

As soon as you have done this, pour slowly into the beaker a little strong *sulphuric acid*. The sugar will almost instantly become black, and will swell up and lose its shape, and in a few minutes will be entirely converted into a black mass: this mass consists almost entirely of charcoal.

You must be very careful not to allow your finger to come in contact with anything that contains sulphuric acid, as will be the case with this black mass, for sulphuric acid corrodes and destroys the skin and flesh almost as easily as it does sugar.

Now, although you cannot understand at present the reason of this curious experiment, you will, I think, be prepared by it to admit the truth of what I told you, namely, that sugar, instead of being an element, or simple substance, is really a compound which contains charcoal, or *carbon*, as it is called by chemists. Besides carbon, sugar contains two gases, which, when combined together, form water, so that sugar may be said to consist of nothing but charcoal and water.

Unfortunately, we cannot, by mixing charcoal and water together, obtain sugar, or possibly it might be more convenient than getting it from sugar-canes.

Now let us try an experiment with another substance. Take a small piece of *blue vitriol;* put it into a test-tube, and pour on it about half a wine-glassful of water. Then heat the test-tube gently over a spirit-lamp, until all, or nearly all, the blue vitriol has dissolved, and the water has consequently assumed a blue colour. Allow the solution (that is, the water in which the blue vitriol has been dissolved) to cool, and pour it into a wine-glass.

When you have done this, dip into the liquid in the wine-glass, a piece of bright steel or iron—a knife-blade will do very well,—and allow it to remain in for a few seconds. When you take it out, you will observe that the portion of it which was immersed in the liquid appears as if it had been converted into copper.

Of course this is not really the case; the iron is only covered with a thin coating of copper, as you may easily see by rubbing the knife-blade with sand-paper, when the red colour will soon disappear.

In this experiment it is evident that as iron is an element, and therefore cannot contain copper, the copper which was deposited on the surface of the knife-blade, could only have come from the blue solution. Blue vitriol, in fact, contains copper, and is therefore not an element, but a compound.

Here then are two substances which appear simple enough, but which are yet found to be compounds when submitted to the test of experiment.

The same thing is true of a great many other substances; and chemists have proceeded in this way, examining or *analysing*, as they call it, first one and then another substance, until they have ascertained the number of the elements to be about sixty-one. I say *about* sixty-one, because the number is frequently altered with the progress of chemistry; and it happens just now that it is not quite certain whether one or two substances are to be regarded as elements or compounds.

The whole object of chemistry is to ascertain the nature and properties of these elements and their compounds, with the laws which govern and control them.

Metallic and Non-Metallic Elements.—The elements have been divided into two great classes,—metallic elements, or metals, and non-metallic elements. You will see, by examining the following table, that you are already familiar with a good many of them; iron, copper, and silver, for instance, among the metals; and sulphur among the non-metallic bodies.

It is not necessary that you should learn this table by heart. I only give it that you may be able to refer to it from time to time.

The letters and numbers which are attached to the names of the elements, you may pass without notice for the present. I hope to make you understand the use of them before long.

Thirteen Non-Metallic Elements.

Oxygen	O.	8	Sulphur	S.	16
Hydrogen	H.	1	Phosphorus	P.	31
Nitrogen	N.	14	Selenium	Se.	39·5
Chlorine	Cl.	35·5	Carbon	C.	6
Bromine	Br.	80	Boron	Bo.	10·9
Iodine	I.	127	Silicon	Si.	21·3
Fluorine	F.	19			

Forty-eight Metallic Elements, or Metals.

Aluminum	Al.	13·7	Molybdenum	Mo.	46
Antimony (*Stibium*)	Sb.	120·6	Nickel	Ni.	29·6
Arsenic	As.	75	Niobium (*Columbium*)	Nb.	
Barium	Ba.	68·5	Osmium	Os.	99·6
Bismuth	Bi.	213	Palladium	Pd.	53·3
Cadmium	Cd.	56·	Platinum	Pt.	98·7
Calcium	Ca.	20	Potassium (*Kalium*)	K.	39
Cerium	Ce.	47	Rhodium	R.	52·2
Chromium	Cr.	26·7	Ruthenium	Ru.	52·2
Cobalt	Co.	29·5	Silver (*Argentum*)	Ag.	108
Copper (*Cuprum*)	Cu.	31·7	Sodium (*Natrium*)	Na.	23
Didymium	D.	48	Strontium	Sr.	43·8
Erbium	E.		Tantalum	T.	184
Glucinum (*Beryllium*)	Gl.	14·1	Tellurium	Te.	64·2
Gold (*Aurum*)	Au.	197	Terbium	Tb.	
Ilmenium	Il.		Thorium	Th.	59·6
Iridium	Ir.	99	Tin (*Stannum*)	Sn.	59
Iron (*Ferrum*)	Fe.	28	Titanium	Ti.	25
Lanthanum	La.	47	Tungsten (*Wolfram*)	W.	95
Lead (*Plumbum*)	Pb.	103·7	Uranium	U.	60
Lithium	Li.	6·5	Vanadium	V.	68·6
Magnesium	Mg.	12	Yttrium	Y.	
Manganese	Mn.	27·6	Zinc	Zn.	32·6
Mercury (*Hydrargyrum*)	Hg.	100	Zirconium	Zr.	33·6

CHAPTER III.

CHEMICAL AFFINITY.

Difference between Mixture and Combination. — TAKE some copper filings, and add to them one third of their weight of sulphur. Stir these ingredients as much as you like, rub them, or pound them in a mortar; still, after all your efforts, the properties of the two substances will remain unchanged; the copper will still be copper, and the sulphur, sulphur; and if you examine the mixture with a magnifying glass, you will see that this is the case, for you will be able to distinguish the red grains of copper and the yellow grains of sulphur.

This is said to be a case of mere *mixture*, and not of combination, because the properties of the constituents were not altered, but only masked, or disguised, by their mixture together.

Now let us present these two elements to one another under different circumstances.

Melt the sulphur by itself in a little earthen crucible of the form shown in fig. 6, *a*.

This may be done either by putting the crucible in a little nook in the fire, or else over a lamp, in the way shown in the cut. In either case, take care that the sulphur does not catch fire.

When it is quite liquid, throw the copper filings

in with the point of a knife, a little at a time. The copper will become red hot, and glow for a second or

Fig. 6.

two, and then disappear. Allow the crucible to cool, and you will find that neither copper nor sulphur is now to be found in it, but only a blackish mass. Reduce this mass to powder in a mortar, and examine it with a magnifying glass. If the proportions were right, neither copper nor sulphur will be detected.

Now, although you cannot see the copper or the sulphur in this black mass, yet both may be discovered in it by chemical means. It is, in fact, a *compound* of those two elements, having properties totally different from either.

You will see, I hope, by this experiment, that a mixture and a compound, or combination, are two very different things. In a mixture, the properties of the substances mixed are not changed, though they may partially disguise one another; but in a compound it generally happens that the properties which it bears are very different from those of any of the substances of which it is composed. For instance: water is *composed* of two gases, oxygen and hydrogen. Now nothing can be more different from water than these two invisible gases, and they may be *mixed* together without producing anything at all resembling water, but when a light is applied to the mixture, they *combine* together with a loud explosion, and the compound, water, is produced.

You see then, that it would be quite incorrect to say that water was a *mixture* of hydrogen and oxygen. It is a *compound* of those gases. Air, on the contrary, is really a mixture of two gases, oxygen and nitrogen, and must not be spoken of as a compound.

You must bear these two terms, mixture and compound, very carefully in mind, for I shall have frequent occasion to use them.

Chemical affinity.—If you have understood what I have been telling you about chemical compounds, it will be very natural for you to wonder why it is that when substances are presented to one another, they sometimes combine, and sometimes only mix. The reason of this is to be found in what is called chemical affinity. All the elements, and most compounds too, have a certain curious liking for, or tendency to combine with, one another. In some cases it is very strong indeed, in others weak and feeble, while in some it is not seen at all. It is this tendency, or liking, which is termed chemical affinity; and you will easily see that this name is given to it because it expresses the affinity, or attraction, which different bodies have for one another.

Here is an experiment to illustrate this.

Take a little *iodine* on the end of a penknife, and put it on a brick, or some other convenient support. Cut off, *under water*, a piece of *phosphorus*, about the size of a small pea. Dry it quickly and carefully with blotting-paper, and put it on the brick, at a short distance from the iodine. Then, with the knife, push the phosphorus until it comes in contact with the iodine. As soon as it does so, the two elements will combine together so eagerly, that they will burst into flame. The substance which is left behind on the brick, is a compound of the two, and is called *iodide of phosphorus*. This is a case of very strong affinity.

Let us try another experiment with two compounds.

Take two wine-glasses. Moisten the inside of one of them with *hydrochloric acid*, and the other with strong *ammonia*, inverting each of the glasses separately for a moment, in order to allow all the liquid to run out, except what adheres to the sides of the glass. Then put the mouths of the two glasses together, as you see them in the cut. Both glasses

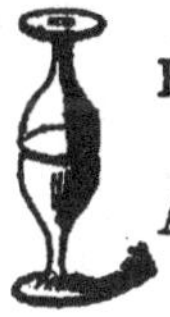

Fig. 7.

will immediately become filled with a dense white vapour, which in a short time will subside into a white powder. The reason of this is, that ammonia and hydrochloric acid have an affinity for one another. When the vapours which each of them give off mix with one another, they combine, and produce the white compound called *chloride of ammonium*.

I have told you that the same substance evinces

different degrees of affinity for other substances. It often happens from this, that when two substances are combined together, and a third is presented to them, which has a more powerful affinity for one of them than they have for one another, the compound is *decomposed.* Here is an instance.

Take a piece of the metal *potassium*, about the size of a pea—you can cut it off very easily with a knife—dry it quickly with blotting-paper, and throw it into a tumbler of water. It will instantly catch fire, and burn, floating all the time on the surface of the water. The reason that it floats is, that, though a metal, it is *lighter than water*.

In this beautiful experiment, the compound, water, is decomposed by the element, potassium.

Water, as I have before mentioned, is a compound of oxygen and hydrogen. Now, although oxygen has a strong affinity for hydrogen, it has a very much stronger affinity for potassium; so that when the potassium is thrown into the water, the oxygen leaves the hydrogen, and combines with the new comer, potassium, just like a man who deserts his old and tried friend to devote his whole affection to a new one. The compound which oxygen forms with potassium is called *potash*. You will understand the whole matter better by examining the following diagram.

Water . . {	Hydrogen	Set free.
	Oxygen———	Potash.
	Potassium———	

Take a tumbler or a bottle, fill it with a pretty strong solution of *acetate of lead*, and, by means of a thread, suspend in it a piece of zinc. Allow the whole to stand for a day or two, and you will find that a beautiful resemblance of vegetation in shining lead has appeared on the zinc. This, which is called

Fig. 8.

the "lead-tree," is due to the fact, that acetic acid, which forms a part of the acetate of lead, has a stronger affinity for zinc than it has for lead.

Double Decomposition.—Sometimes, when two compounds are presented to one another, they mutually decompose one another, and form two fresh compounds.

Half fill a wine-glass with solution of acetate of lead. Then pour into it a little solution of *bichromate of potash.* A beautiful yellow colour is produced, which soon settles down to the bottom of the glass as a yellow powder.

Whenever a solid appears in this way in a liquid, it is called a *precipitate.*

This is a term of very frequent occurrence, and it is therefore important for you to remember it. It is not exclusively applied to substances which settle down easily as the yellow powder now produced does. Some precipitates are so small that they only produce a faint turbidity, or cloudiness in the liquid and only subside after long standing.

Whenever a liquid is not *perfectly clear*, you may be sure that a solid is suspended mechanically in it.

To return to the experiment before us. You will understand the reason of it, if you examine the following diagram.

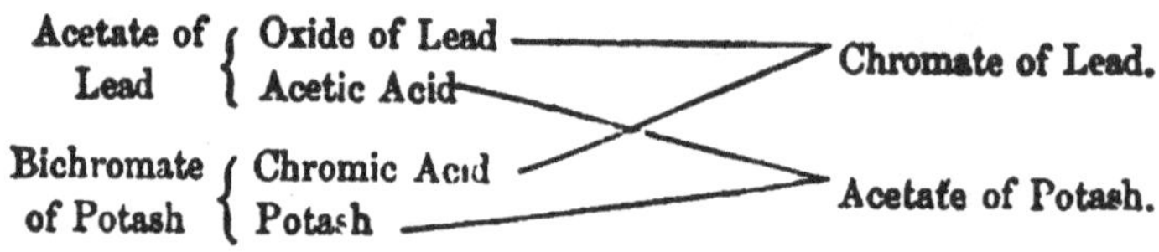

Acetate of lead consists of acetic acid and oxide of lead; bichromate of potash, of chromic acid and potash.

Chromic acid has a strong affinity for oxide of lead, it therefore leaves the potash, and combines with the oxide of lead, which it takes from the acetate of lead. The acetic acid and potash, being both set at liberty, combine with one another, and form acetate of potash. This double change is called an instance of *double decomposition*.

Acids, Bases, and Salts.—I have several times used the word acid, and as I shall have frequent occasion to do so again, I think it will be as well if I explain the meaning of the term before I go any farther. There is a peculiar blue vegetable substance, called *litmus*, which has the property of becoming red in the presence of any acid, and papers stained with this blue litmus are consequently used to test for, or ascertain the presence of an acid. They are called "Test-papers."

Well then, the chemical definition of an acid is this. A substance which is sour to the taste, turns blue litmus red, and combines with *bases* to form *salts*.

The two first of these characteristics are plain enough. You can try them both for yourself with common vinegar, which consists principally of acetic acid. You already know its sour taste, and if you dip a piece of blue litmus paper in it, the paper will be turned red. To enable you to understand the third property of acids I must tell you what is meant by a base.

A base is, in chemical language, the exact reverse of an acid. It is a substance which turns red litmus, or litmus which has been reddened by an acid, back again to blue, and combines with acids, neutralising them, or destroying their acid properties, and producing *salts*. The bases are all *metallic oxides*, or compounds of metals with oxygen. Potash, soda, lime, and oxide of lead are instances. Dip the litmus paper which you reddened with vinegar, into a little solution of potash in a wine-glass. The blue colour is immediately restored.

When I say that the combination together of acids and bases produces *salts*, I do not mean that either common salt, or smelling-salts, is always produced. 'Salt' is the chemical term for any substance which contains an acid and a base, and most salts are very different from either of those substances. Thus, in chemical language, chalk, sugar of lead, sulphate of copper, and corrosive sublimate, are all salts, as well as common salt and smelling-salts.

Litmus is not the only vegetable substance the colour of which is changed by acids and bases.

Take a red cabbage. Cut it in slices, and pour boiling water on a portion of these slices. You will get a blue infusion.

Now take four tumblers, arrange them in a row on the table, and put into the first a few drops of sulphuric acid; into the second, a few drops of solution of potash; into the third, a little solution of alum; while the fourth remains empty. Fill all the tumblers with the tincture of cabbage. In the one containing sulphuric acid it will become *red*, with the potash, *green*, and with the alum, *purple*, while in the remaining tumbler the blue colour is unchanged. You thus get no less than four distinct colours from this one infusion! If you add potash very slowly to the red solution, the colour will change, first back to blue and then to green, the base neutralising the acid, and then acting on the vegetable colour. On the other hand, if to the green solution, sulphuric acid be gradually added, the colour will change, first to blue, and then to red.

CHAPTER IV.

OXYGEN.

O = 8.

Preparation.—ALTHOUGH a few of the elements are to be found in nature in a free or uncombined state, it more often happens that we have to separate them from some one of their combinations before we can obtain them in a state of purity. This is the case with oxygen; for though there is such an immense quantity of it in the world—such a quantity, indeed, that it is supposed that one third of the entire world consists of it—yet, when we wish to prepare it, we have to separate it from substances which contain it.

Fit a small hard-glass test-tube with a cork. Take a piece of glass tubing about one quarter of an inch wide, and cut off from one end of it, a piece a foot in length.

The way in which glass tubes and rods are cut is this.

At the point where you wish to divide it, make a sharp, quick scratch or two with a small file. Then take the tube in both hands, and try to bend it at the point opposite to the scratch. You will find that it breaks off quite easily, and with a perfectly smooth and even edge. In fig. 9, *a* is the point where the scratch is made. The piece of tubing so cut off is now to be bent to shape shown in fig. 10. This is done by holding the tube in the upper part of the flame of a spirit-lamp, with both hands, until it softens at the point you wish, and then bending it slowly upwards with your fore-finger.

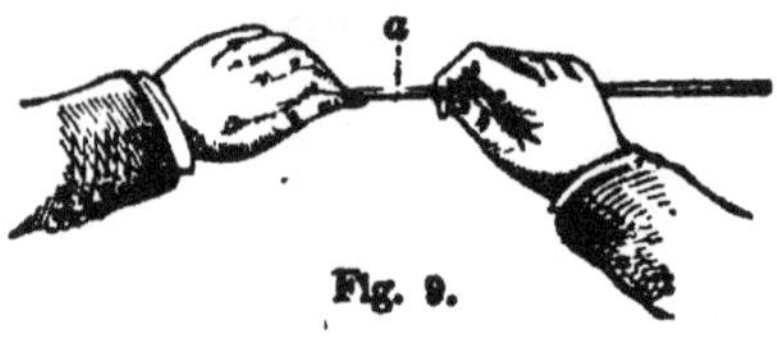

Fig. 9.

When you have done this, bore a hole in the cork which fits your test-tube, with that one out of the set of cork-borers* which corresponds best to the size of the long tube. If you have no cork-borers, you must use a small round file, which may be bought for about threepence. When the hole is made, pass the end of the tube through the cork, and replace the cork in the test tube. The apparatus now appears as you see it in fig. 10.

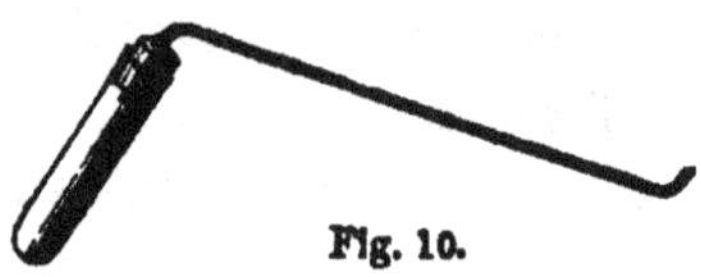

Fig. 10.

When this is ready, put into the test-tube a little *red oxide of mercury*—enough to fill about half an inch of it—and replace the cork and tube. When this is done, support the tube over the edge of a washhand-basin which is about half full of water, allowing the long tube to dip below the surface. Fill a test-tube with water, and support, or hold it, with its mouth

* Cork-borers are short pieces of brass tube, sharpened at the end. They are sold in sets.

downwards, just over the open end of the tube, but still under the water. Put a spirit-lamp under the

Fig. 11.

test-tube, and heat the substance in it strongly. After a time, bubbles of gas will begin to rise through the water into the inverted test-tube, and will soon fill it.

When this is the case, remove the *retort*, as the apparatus containing the oxide of mercury is called, from the water, taking care not to allow the mouth of the tube which contains the gas to rise above the water. Put your left hand under the water, and cover the mouth of the tube with your thumb, so that you can take it out of the water without the gas escaping. Have ready a wooden match, light it, and allow it to burn for a second or two, then blow it out, and plunge it into the tube of gas before the red-hot end has gone out. The match will be immediately rekindled, and will burn for an instant with far greater brilliancy than it did in the air.

It is evident that there was something in the tube different from common air. This something is oxygen gas.

Now for the explanation of this experiment. If you look in the inside of the tube in which the oxide of mercury was heated, you will perceive that there are a number of bright globules of metallic quicksilver, or mercury, adhering to the glass. This makes the reason of the oxygen being evolved quite evident. Oxide of mercury is a compound of mercury and oxygen. The affinity between these two elements is overcome by the heat applied, and the oxygen is given off, while the mercury is deposited on the sides of the tube.

Now this experiment, though a very instructive one, does not furnish us with a convenient process for preparing oxygen in quantities. I shall now describe a better one.

Make a tube-retort, similar to that used in the last experiment, but with a test-tube six inches long and one inch wide, and a bent tube, or "delivery-tube," as it is called, rather larger than the one you used before. Reduce to powder some *chlorate of potash* with a mortar and pestle, and mix with it about an equal quantity of powdered *binoxide of manganese*, which must be previously dried in an iron shovel over a fire or lamp.

This mixture of chlorate of potash and binoxide of manganese is called "oxygen composition," and it affords a ready means of procuring oxygen gas. Many other substances may be used, but this is by far the most convenient.

Fill the retort you have made, about one-third full of the oxygen composition, and then your apparatus is ready.

Pneumatic Trough.—Before you make the gas, I must tell you a little more about the method of collecting gases which is generally employed.

Dr. Priestley, the discoverer of oxygen, was the first who made use of the apparatus called the *pneumatic trough*, which is represented in the annexed cut.

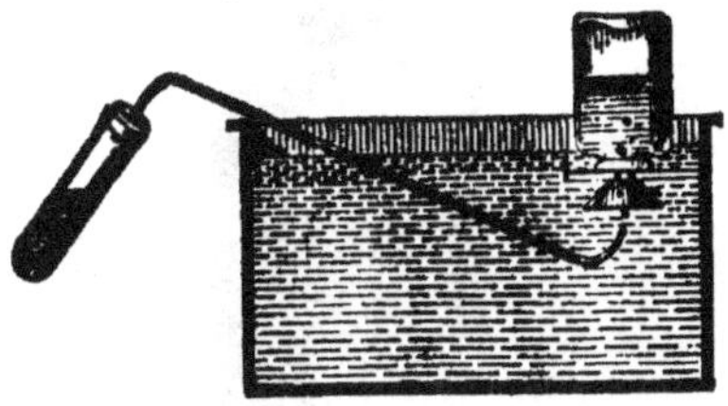

Fig. 12.

It consists of an oblong box, generally made of japanned tin, or of wood, with a shelf across one end, and one or two inches from the top. This box is filled with water till the shelf is completely covered, and the bottles, or jars, which are to be filled with gas, are first filled with water, and inverted on the shelf in the manner shown in the drawing.

In the shelf are one or two holes, and attached to the holes underneath are small tin funnels, to collect the bubbles of gas. When the end of the delivery-tube is put under one of these funnels, and the bottle full of water on the shelf exactly above it, it is evident that the gas in passing from the delivery-tube will bubble up through the water, and fill the bottle. When the bottle is full, it may be slid gently off the shelf, and the stopper replaced while the mouth is yet under water. If, instead of a bottle, the vessel to be filled be a jar, open at the bottom, it may be removed from the trough when full, by sliding it off the shelf on to a plate held below the water. The plate with the jar on it may then be raised out of the trough, and the gas cannot escape, because the water remaining in the plate prevents it from passing.

Fig. 13.

Sometimes it happens that you require to transfer gas from one bottle or jar into another. This can be done very conveniently in the pneumatic trough in the following manner.

Fig. 14.

The bottle into which you wish to transfer the gas is filled with water, and inverted in the trough by the side of the bottle containing the gas. The latter is then slowly tilted up, with its mouth just below the other bottle, when the gas will bubble up into it by a kind of inverse pouring. The arrangement is shown in fig. 14.

Now although this is on the whole the most convenient form of pneumatic trough, there are simpler and cheaper contrivances which answer very well for small quantities. In making oxygen from oxide of mercury, you used a washhand-basin for a trough. A better thing than this is a small foot-pan; and this, with the addition of a *bee-hive shelf*, is perhaps as good as any other. The bee-hive shelf is a little piece of apparatus, made usually of stoneware, which can be used in almost any shallow vessel, to support a bottle or small jar. You will see by the drawing (fig. 15) that it has two holes, one at the side to admit the delivery tube, and another at the top to allow the gas to pass into the bottle. It is bell-shaped inside, and is of course to be completely covered with water. A section of it is shown at *a*.

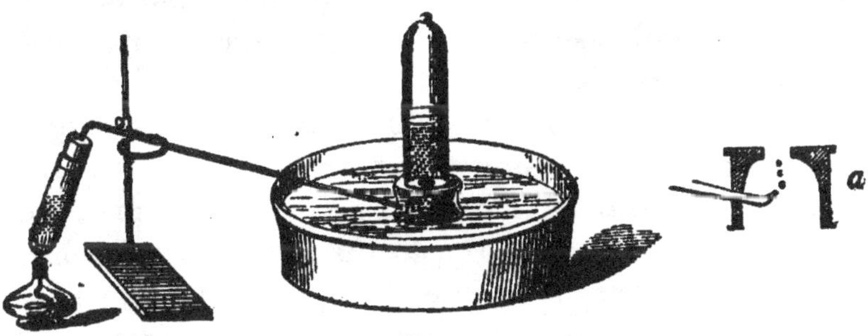

Fig. 15.

Whichever pneumatic trough you use, the way of working with it is the same; but as it is the cheapest, I will suppose you are going to use the bee-hive shelf.

The next thing to get ready is something to collect the gas in. You should have one stoppered gas-jar, though a stoppered bottle with the bottom out will do instead; but for most experiments bottles answer as well or better. The sort of bottle that you want is a wide-mouthed stoppered one, that will hold about a pint of water; but one rather smaller will do.

You must have at least three or four of these, though if you cannot get them, it is possible to manage with bottles without stoppers, by keeping the bottle containing the gas, bottom upwards in a cup or plate containing water, in the same way as the gas-jar, as represented in fig. 13.

Before you begin to use them, the stopper of each bottle should be smeared with a very little lard or pomatum, and then turned round a few times in the neck of the bottle, so as to spread the grease uniformly. The object of this is to make the stopper *gas-tight*, and also to prevent any chance of its sticking in the bottle.

Now arrange the tube-retort containing the oxygen mixture in the manner represented in fig. 15, and apply the heat of a spirit-lamp, gently at first, but afterwards more strongly, to the test-tube. Bubbles of gas will very soon rise through the water, and as the heat increases, they will come over in a most rapid and violent manner. As soon as one bottle is full, slide it quickly off the shelf, insert its stopper, under water, and remove it; then, as quickly as possible, replace it on the shelf by another bottle.

Proceed in this way until all your bottles are full, or till no more gas is given off from the mixture. Then remove the end of the delivery-tube from the water, and *afterwards* take away the spirit-lamp, and let the retort get cold. I tell you to take the tube out of the water before you remove the spirit-lamp, because the gas in the tube, in common with all other gases, has the curious property of being expanded, or increased in bulk, by heat. The effect of this very important fact, in the present case, would be, that if you allowed the tube-retort to cool while the delivery-tube was under water, the gas in the apparatus would contract, or shrink up, and the water out of the trough would rush back to occupy its place, and would very likely crack the glass.*

You have now collected a considerable quantity of oxygen gas. The next thing is to examine a little into its properties.

Experiment 1.—Take a bottle of oxygen. Have ready a piece of wax taper, bent into this form J. Light this at the shorter end, and allow it to burn until the wick remains red hot when you blow it out. As soon as this is the case, take the stopper out of the bottle, and plunge into it the lighted taper. The taper will burn much more brightly than it did in the air. Take the taper out almost immediately, blow it out, and put it back in the bottle; it will instantly rekindle, with a little pop, and will burn as brightly as before. In a minute or so, all the oxygen will be exhausted, and then the taper will probably go out. You will learn the reason of this by-and-by.

We learn from this experiment two very important facts. The first of these is, that oxygen is not a *combustible* body; that is, it will not burn. You observed that though the taper burnt so brightly itself, it did

* The explanation of this process is given at page 92.

not set the oxygen alight, as it would have done with common coal gas, for instance. The second, and the most important of all the properties of oxygen, is, that it is a powerful *supporter of combustion*. I think I need hardly explain what this means. Combustion, as you probably know, means burning; so that the term supporter of combustion simply implies that it is a supporter of the burning of other bodies, and this the experiment with the taper very clearly proves.

Experiment 2.—Choose out a small piece of barky charcoal; tie this with thin copper wire to a thick iron wire about ten inches long, and pass one end of this wire through a broad thin bung. Slide the bung along the wire until the charcoal is at such a distance from it, that when dipped into a bottle, the charcoal would be about in the middle of it. Hold the charcoal in a spirit-lamp, until one end is thoroughly alight, and then plunge it into a bottle of oxygen, allowing the bung to rest on the neck of the bottle.

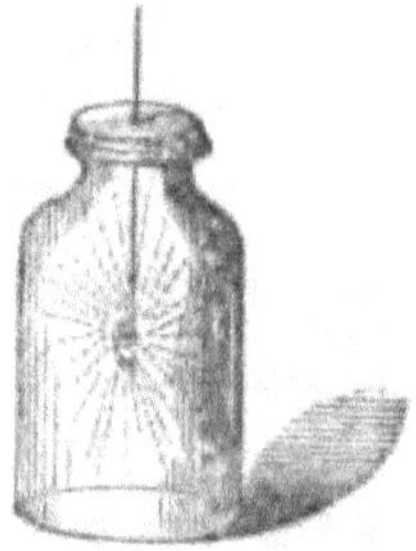

Fig. 16.

The charcoal will burn brilliantly, and if there be much bark on it, will throw out the most beautiful sparks in all directions. If you had sufficient oxygen, you might go on till all the charcoal was consumed, and nothing remained of it but a very little white ash; but it generally happens that there is not nearly enough oxygen, the oxygen disappearing very rapidly in proportion to the small size of the charcoal which consumes it.

We see then, that two elements, oxygen and carbon, which, as I have before told you, is almost the same as charcoal, are disappearing during this experiment. What then, we may naturally ask, becomes of them? Are they destroyed — struck out of the book of creation altogether? or are they only hidden away for a time, in some new and unsuspected shape, to reappear in due season, and play their parts as before? Though at first sight it would hardly appear so, yet this is the more probable view, even apart from chemical investigations; for when we think how much fire and burning there has been on this earth since God created it, and that on a scale which makes even the mightiest conflagrations produced by men's hands altogether insignificant; the tremendous volcanoes which have been, and still are, at work, melting and boiling the solid rocks themselves, and strewing their Cyclopean relics in every corner of the world; we cannot but be struck by the idea that, were it possible for the elements to be destroyed by fire, such gigantic burnings as these would, in the long course of ages, have greatly diminished and dwindled the original size which was imparted to our planet. This is of course very improbable.

But there is no lack of chemical evidence on the

subject — clear, unmistakable, and complete. No element can possibly, unless God were to alter the laws which He himself has appointed, be destroyed or lost. Whenever, as in the case before us, it appears that such is the case, we may rest assured that the elements concerned are but passing into some new shape, or combination, from which they may be reproduced by suitable means. Let us now see if we can understand what has become of the carbon and oxygen. They have combined together by virtue of chemical affinity, and have produced an acid compound, which is well known by the name of carbonic acid gas. You can prove this very simply for yourselves.

1. Take a piece of blue litmus paper, and moisten it with the few drops of water which remained in the bottle when you filled it with oxygen. You will see that the test-paper is reddened. This, you will remember, is a proof that *an acid* is present (v. page 23).

2. Prepare a little *lime-water*. This is done by putting a little quick, or recently slaked, lime into a bottle full of distilled water, and allowing them to remain in contact for some hours, shaking the bottle every now and then. The water dissolves a little of the lime, and as soon as it is *saturated*, that is, as soon as the water will dissolve no more lime, you can pour as much as possible of the clear liquid off into another bottle. This clear liquid is the lime-water, and it is said to be a *test* for free or uncombined carbonic acid, because it is used to detect the presence of that gas in the way you will now see.

Into the bottle in which you burned the charcoal, and in which you have just dipped the test-paper, pour about a wine-glassful of lime-water; put the stopper in, and shake the bottle, with the lime-water, in it. In a minute, the lime-water, which before was perfectly clear and transparent, will become white and milky-looking.

Now whenever lime-water assumes this milky look on being shaken with a gas, we always know that carbonic acid is present, and this is why lime-water is called a *test* for carbonic acid.

The reason of the milky appearance is, that the *acid*, carbonic acid, combines with the *base*, lime, and forms the *salt*, carbonate of lime (p. 23), which is insoluble in water. This carbonate of lime is the same in composition as common chalk and marble.

Experiment 3.—Take a deflagrating spoon. This is a little brass ladle, attached to the end of an iron

Fig. 17.

wire. It is very commonly used for burning things in gases, for which purpose it is best to push the wire through a flat bung, protected on the lower side by a piece of tin-plate, which may prevent the gas from passing out of the bottle.

Put into this spoon a piece of sulphur, or brimstone, as it is sometimes called, about the size of a large pea. Hold the spoon in the flame of a spirit-lamp, until the sulphur is melted and begins to burn; slide the bung until it is at the height shown in fig. 17, and then, the sulphur being thoroughly alight, plunge it into a bottle of oxygen gas.

The sulphur will burn very brightly, and with a beautiful blue flame.

In this experiment, like the last, the oxygen combines with the sulphur to form an acid. A gas remains in the bottle when the sulphur has ceased to burn, which, when examined, is found to be a compound of sulphur and oxygen. This compound is called *sulphurous acid*, and it is the same substance which produces the disagreeable smell when lucifer matches with sulphur on them are burnt. It is soluble in water, so that if there be any water in the bottle, the gas will soon be absorbed.

Experiment 4.—Instead of the sulphur used in the last experiment, take a rather smaller piece of dry phosphorus. This will burn in a bottle of oxygen, with a most magnificent white flame, and the bottle will remain filled with dense white fumes.

These fumes consist of *phosphoric acid*, and, like *sulphurous acid*, they are soluble in water.

Experiment 5.—In all the cases which you have yet seen, acid compounds have been produced by the combustion of substances in oxygen. But this is not always the case, for sometimes it happens that either a base or a neutral body, that is, a body which is neither an acid nor a base, is produced. Then again, in all the preceding cases, the substances were capable of burning, even in the air, though they burnt more brightly in oxygen. I will now give you an experiment which differs in both these respects from those you have done before.

Take a very small and thin watch-spring—you can get a broken one at any watchmaker's for almost nothing—heat this red hot, and let it cool again, so as to soften it, and then bend it straight. Break off a piece about eight inches long, and pass it through a bung, just as you do the deflagrating spoons, but far enough to reach to within an inch and a half of the bottom of a stoppered gas jar. This gas jar must be filled with oxygen, and be standing on a plate filled with water (fig. 13). The bottom end of the watch-spring is then to be made hot, and dipped into some powdered sulphur, so that some of the sulphur adheres to it. When this is done, light the sulphur at the end of the watch-spring, and plunge it into the jar of gas, through the neck. The sulphur burns for a second or two, and then sets light to the iron. You can see the end of the iron boiling and burning, and throwing out the most beautiful sparks, while every now and then a white-hot drop falls, and becomes firmly fixed into the plate, even after passing through the water. If there be enough oxygen, the whole of the watch-spring which is inside the jar will be burnt. At the end of the experiment, besides the black shining globules which are in the plate and at the end of the watch-spring, you will find that the inside of the jar is covered with a red powder. This red powder, which is the same as common red rust, is a compound of oxygen and iron, and is called oxide of iron. It is a *base*. The black globules consist of a compound of oxygen and iron in different proportions from the red oxide. This last oxide is a *neutral body*.

Experiment 6.—Take a very small bottle of oxygen, one four inches high, and an inch and a half across, will do. Take out the stopper, and pour in two or three drops of *bisulphide of carbon*. This is a very dangerous and inflamable liquid, so that you must use it with great care, and not on any account allow it to come near a light. When you have poured in the bisulphide of carbon, replace the stopper, and shake it with the oxygen, so as to allow its vapour to become mixed with the latter. Then place the bottle on a table at some distance from you, take out the stopper, and instantly apply a light to the mouth, or else dip into it a bent and nearly red-hot iron wire. A sharp explosion will follow, attended with a flash of light. A little free sulphur from the bisulphide of carbon is deposited on the inside of the bottle.

Experiment 7.—In the preceding experiments you have prepared the oxygen first, and then presented other bodies to it. I will now show you that oxygen, even when it is in the act of being given off, will sometimes combine with other substances, and produce flame. Nitre, or saltpetre (nitrate of potash), is a salt which, when heated, gives off oxygen,

Take some of this salt in a small iron ladle, melt it over a common fire, and when it is very hot throw in a small cinder or a little charcoal powder. In either case there will be a beautiful combustion, and in the latter a shower of sparks.

The same experiment may be performed with a small piece of sulphur instead of a cinder.

Experiment 8.—Melt some zinc in an iron ladle, and when it is very hot, hold it under a chimney, and throw in a little powdered nitre. The oxygen given off by the nitre, will cause the zinc to burn with a most beautiful white light, while flakes of white oxide of zinc float about above the ladle, and are soon deposited.

Nature of combustion.—One of the very first things I told you was, that fire, which was generally spoken of as an element, was not a substance, but only an effect. Its real nature we know scarcely anything about, but we find that when two substances have a strong affinity for one another, and combine rapidly together, fire, that is light and heat, very frequently results.

You have already had a good many instances of this—the iodine and phosphorus, for instance (page 19), as well as the various bodies which you have burned in oxygen; for though they did not commence burning until a light was applied to them, they continued to burn very brightly indeed when once lit.

Combustion then, you must remember, is the term given to the combination of different bodies together, when that combination is attended with light and heat. This is the true meaning of the word, though in practice it is generally confined to the combination of bodies with oxygen, or the *oxidation* of bodies at high temperatures.

The air, as you remember I told you before (v. page 18), is a mixture of two gases—oxygen and nitrogen. When any substance, such as a candle, or a piece of coal, burns in the air, it combines with the oxygen of the air just as though it had been burnt in oxygen gas, though not so quickly or brightly. The nitrogen, as you will see hereafter, is not changed, but acts simply in *diluting*, as it were, the oxygen, and preventing its too violent action.

All fuel consists mainly of carbon, generally combined with a smaller and variable quantity of hydrogen. Now you saw just now (v. page 36) that when carbon combines with oxygen, the substance called carbonic acid is produced. This is just what happens both with fires and candles. The carbon contained in the coals and in the tallow, is *oxidized* by the oxygen of the air, and carbonic acid, which is a gas, goes up the chimney in the case of a fire, or escapes into the air of the room when it is a candle or lamp which is burning.

Respiration.—The process of combustion, which I have just been describing to you, bears, strange to say, a very close resemblance to another process which is constantly going on within our bodies—the process of respiration. When we draw air into our lungs, as we do in breathing, we cause the oxygen to come into very close contact with the impure blood, which, after traversing the most distant parts of the body, has returned to the lungs. This blood, besides water, consists mainly of carbon. A portion of this carbon combines with the oxygen and forms carbonic acid, which is breathed out again into the air, while enough heat is given off by the carbon in oxidizing, to impart to the body the heat which it always possesses, and which is necessary to support life.

You see that all this is very much like a lamp or candle burning in the air; and these are not the only points of similarity, for just as a lamp would soon go out if no fresh supply of oil were given to it, so if the waste caused by this constant oxidation of a portion of the body were not compensated for by the food we eat, our life would soon come to an end. The oxygen would burn a great part of the flesh of our bodies way, and before death put an end to our sufferings we should become miserably thin, and very much reduced in weight. This we find is actually the case when anybody is starved to death. The simile of the lamp of life being extinguished in death, is, you see, an almost literal truth.

Other properties of oxygen.—Oxygen gas is colourless, and without taste or smell. It is rather heavier than air, and is only very slightly soluble in water. It is capable of combining with all the other elements with the exception of fluorine. The compounds which it forms with them are called *oxides*, and, as I have already mentioned, they are divided into three classes:—

1. Acid Oxides, or Acids—*e.g.*, Carbonic Acid, Nitric Acid, Sulphuric Acid.
2. Basic Oxides, or Bases—*e.g.*, Protoxide of iron, Oxide of Potassium (potash).
3. Neutral Oxides—*e.g.*, Binoxide of Manganese, Protoxide of Nitrogen.

OZONE.

Take a stoppered bottle; put into it a stick of phosphorus; half cover this with water, and rest the stopper loosely on the neck of the bottle. Allow the whole to stand for two or three hours, and then remove the phosphorus.

During this time a little of the phosphorus will have become oxidized at the expense of the air, and the remaining oxygen will be found to have acquired a peculiar smell, and properties differing materially from common oxygen. This is because a portion of it has been converted into *ozone*. Ozone is perfectly pure oxygen; it only differs from common oxygen in its properties, and it therefore presents a curious instance of what is called *allotropy*. When a substance is capable of existing in two or more different states, without any alteration in its composition, those various states, or forms, are called "allotropic." Thus, in the present instance, ozone is called "allotropic oxygen."

Ozone has never yet been obtained in a pure state —it is always mixed with common oxygen. It is far more energetic in combining with other bodies than ordinary oxygen, many bodies which are not affected by the latter, being readily decomposed by ozone.

Mix a solution of starch with a little solution of iodide of potassium. No effect is produced. Now pour the mixture into the bottle containing the ozonized air, and a blue colour will be immediately produced (v. page 98).

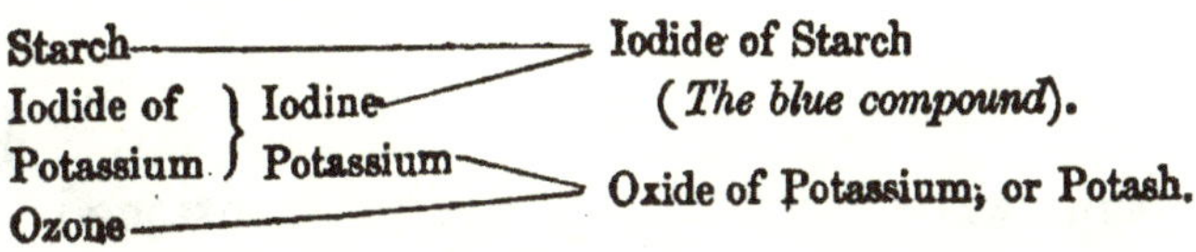

The ozone combines with the iodine of the iodide of potassium, and forms with it potash, for ozone when it combines with another body produces the same compound as if it had been common oxygen.

Ozone possesses very powerful bleaching properties. A little infusion of logwood or Brazil-wood, poured into a bottle of ozonized air, and shaken, will almost immediately lose its colour.

Ozone is very frequently found in the air, where it appears to be formed by the passage of electricity during thunder-storms.

Sea-air generally contains more ozone than the air of inland countries, and this is supposed by some to be the cause of the greater healthiness of the former.

CHAPTER V.

HYDROGEN.

H = 1.

Preparation.—I HAVE repeatedly mentioned that water contains, besides oxygen, another gas called hydrogen. This gas, which is one of the most important of the elements, is almost always procured from water, though the way in which it is obtained varies very much. I will describe the most convenient process.

Take a wide-mouthed bottle capable of holding about half a pint. Fit it with a tight cork, and bore two holes through the cork. One of these holes is to contain a long, thistle-headed funnel. This is nothing but a tube with an enlargement at one end to allow of liquids being poured easily through it. Into the other hole fit a tube, previously bent to the shape shown at *d* in fig. 18.

Cover the bottom of the bottle to the depth of about half an inch with *granulated zinc.* This is zinc which has been melted in a ladle, and poured, while melting, into cold water, in a pail or other vessel. It is in very sharp, irregular-shaped pieces. Replace the cork *b*, with the two tubes in it, in the bottle, allowing the thistle-funnel to pass very nearly to the bottom. This first bottle is called the "generator," because in it the gas is prepared, or generated.

You require a second bottle, in which to wash the gas after it leaves the generator, in order to render it purer. This is rather smaller than the generator, and has two tubes, the shapes of which are shown at *e* in the figure. The first of them passes down to the bottom of the bottle, so that when the bottle is half filled with water, the gas, in issuing from the generator, has to bubble up through the water. The two bottles are best connected by means of a short piece of vulcanized india-rubber tubing; this is shown at *g*. The delivery-tube *f* may likewise be made of this vulcanized tubing, though glass does nearly as well.

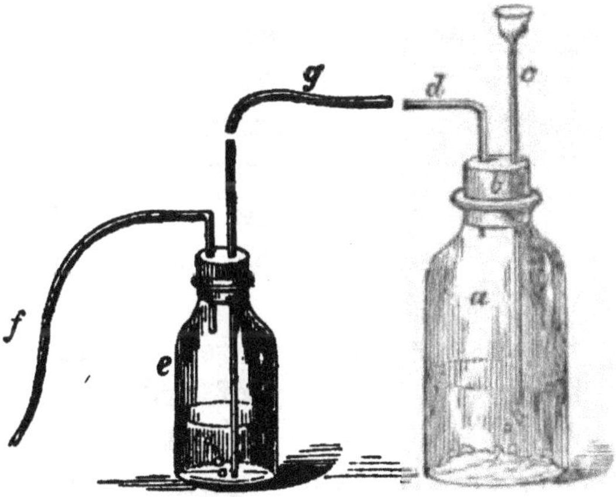

Fig. 18.—*a* is the generator; *b* the cork; *c* the thistle-funnel; *d* the bent tube; *e* the wash-bottle; *f* the delivery-tube; *g* the connector.

Well then, this apparatus being all ready, water having been put into the second, or *wash-bottle*, and zinc into the generator, water is to be poured into the latter through the long funnel, until the bottle is about one-quarter full. Sulphuric acid is then to be poured down the funnel—not too much at first—

perhaps about half a wine-glassful. In a very few minutes, gas begins to rise in the generator. This passes along the tube *d*, and bubbles up through the water in the wash-bottle, and so passes out through the delivery-tube.*

The gas is to be collected over water in the pneumatic trough, exactly in the same way that oxygen was; but before you attempt to do so, I have a most important caution to give you. Do not collect the first gas which comes over. Even when the gas is bubbling quickly through the water in the wash-bottle, you must wait a few minutes before you attempt to collect any. The reason that this is necessary is, that the apparatus contains at starting a good deal of common air, so that the first portions of gas which come over are not hydrogen, but a mixture of hydrogen and common air. This mixture, as you will presently see, is very explosive. When the gas has passed out for a few minutes, it will have driven all the common air out, and then the pure hydrogen may be collected.

Properties.—I will now suppose you to have collected some bottles and jars of hydrogen, and will proceed to show you how to illustrate its properties.

It is combustible, but not a supporter of combustion.—Take a bottle of the gas: hold it with its mouth downwards, and take out the stopper. Then take a straight piece of taper, light it, and pass it up into the bottle. You will observe that as you do so the gas will burst into flame at the mouth of the bottle,

* You cannot at present understand the reason of this process. You will find it fully explained at page 86.

but that the taper will be extinguished. If you now draw the taper slowly out, it will be relighted by the burning hydrogen at the mouth of the bottle, but may be again extinguished by passing it up into the gas.

It is a very light gas.—In the last experiment, you were directed to open the bottle of gas with its *mouth downwards.* The reason that this is necessary is, that hydrogen is such a very light gas, that if the bottle were held in the usual way, the gas would soon ascend out of it, and common air take its place. Take a bottle of the gas, hold it with its mouth upwards, remove the stopper, and allow it to stand for a minute or two. Then dip a taper into it, and you will find that all the hydrogen has escaped, and that the taper consequently burns without change. If the bottle had been held mouth-downwards, as in the previous experiment, the gas would have remained a much longer time before it escaped; but even then it would ultimately have done so.

Collecting by displacement.—One curious effect of this lightness of hydrogen is, that we are enabled to collect it without using the pneumatic trough, by a process which is called *displacement.*

Take the delivery-tube out of the wash-bottle *e*, fig. 18, and substitute for it a straight glass tube, eight or nine inches long. Prepare the hydrogen in the generator *a* just as you did before. When the common air has been expelled from the apparatus, hold an empty bottle over the long delivery-tube (fig. 19 *h*). The mouth of the bottle had better be roughly closed by a card with a hole in it, *i*, to allow the tube to pass through. This is a precaution which it is wise to take whenever a gas is collected by displacement.

Fig. 19.

The light gas will rise through the heavier air for just the same reason that a cork will rise through water, and in a very short time will completely fill the bottle. It is rather difficult to judge when this is the case. If the gas be coming off pretty rapidly, it will not take more than a few minutes. When you consider it to be full, remove the bottle by raising it slowly, and apply a light: the gas will burn as it did in the first experiment.

Balloons.—It is to the lightness of hydrogen gas that *gas-balloons* owe their power of rising in the air. If a bag be filled with hydrogen, or any other gas, and the weight of the bag when filled, be less than the weight of an equal bulk of air, it will rise, and the heavier air above it will descend to take its place. This is what is actually the case with balloons. If you can procure a little balloon of *gold-*

beaters' skin, which may be had for about two shillings, you can illustrate this very well for yourself. You must proceed in the following manner:—

Put a little piece of cotton-wool in the lower end of the delivery-tube in fig. 20, in order to absorb

Fig. 20.

any water which may condense from the gas. Empty the balloon as much as possible, by pressing it with your hands, and tie its mouth with fine silk on to the upper end of the delivery-tube. Make the hydrogen as usual, but be sure to let the greater part, at any rate, of the common air escape before you tie on the balloon. The gas will gradually cause the little balloon to swell out, and will soon fill it. When this is the case, slip its mouth off the end of the glass tube, and instantly tie it tightly with the silk, so that no gas can escape. If it be now left to itself, it will rise rapidly to the ceiling of the room, and will remain there for some little time; but at last it will descend, because the gas will pass slowly through the bag.

There are two kinds of balloons, the gas-balloon, and the fire-balloon. Gas-balloons were for a long time filled with hydrogen, but now coal gas is always employed, as being cheaper and more convenient; although, from its greater weight, it renders it necessary to have the balloon much larger. The fire-balloon is open at the bottom, and is kept full of hot air by something burning in its mouth. Hot air is lighter than cold air, and so the balloon rises.

The first balloon in which human beings ventured themselves, was one of these fire-balloons. It was made by a man of the name of Montgolfier, and ascended safely from the neighbourhood of Paris, on the 21st November, 1783. It is easy to imagine what an immense excitement was produced by the event. To use the words of the official account, signed by the celebrated Benjamin Franklin and some others, "No one could help feeling a mingled sentiment of fear and admiration." In less than one month after this, a successful ascent was accomplished by two brothers, in a balloon filled with hydrogen gas.

Other Properties of Hydrogen.—As it is generally prepared, hydrogen gas contains some impurities which give it a peculiar and disagreeable smell. When quite pure, it has no smell and no taste: it is quite colourless, and is not poisonous, although it will not support animal life like oxygen does. It has a very peculiar effect upon *sound*. When any musical instrument is played in it, the ordinary tones are entirely lost, and instead of them we get a set of the most singular squeaks imaginable. In the same way, if a person with a bass voice inhales the gas, the bass notes are changed into a nasal squeaking treble. You must on no account attempt to try this experiment, as it would be highly dangerous.

WATER, H O = 9.

By far the most important fact about hydrogen is, that when it combines with oxygen, water is the result. It is totally impossible for us even to conceive the importance of the part which this common liquid plays in every department of life. Even in the circumstances in which its agency is most striking, we find it very hard to realize its full value. Not only do we drink it, not only do we wash in it, not only does it enter into almost every detail of those arts of cooking by which our food is made fit for us and our lives preserved, but we have made that vast reservoir of it—the sea—to be almost as plain and as much frequented as a heathy common; and, not contented with this, we have, as the old magicians were said to do, pressed into our service as our slave, the vapour, or "spirit," as it would formerly have been called, of this same water; compelled it to work day and night for our convenience, and to bear us hither and thither on the broad and deep-blue bosom of its majestic parent. Its importance to us in many other respects is not less striking, though it is less apparent.

You have already seen that its removal from sugar is enough to destroy the before valuable properties of that substance. In like manner, if we deprive meat of all the water which it contains, we have left only one fourth the quantity, of a dry, tasteless, and horn-like substance, entirely unfit for food. Not less than three fourths of the substance of animals and vegetables consist of water, which gave rise to the remark of the great chemist, Liebig, that man's body might fairly be represented by a bucket of water, with a lump of chalk and another of charcoal. I think you will agree with me that this beats Plato's celebrated definition of man, as "a two-legged animal without feathers."

I have told you that water is composed of hydrogen and oxygen. You can prove this in two ways: firstly, by causing oxygen to combine with hydrogen, which is called proving it by *synthesis*; and secondly, by decomposing or dividing the water into its component gases. This last process is called *analysis*. These two terms are of such constant occurrence that I shall take this opportunity of giving you definitions of them.

When the composition of a substance is ascertained by decomposing, or dividing it into its constituent parts, the process is called analysis, and the substance is said to be analysed.

When a compound body is formed by the union together of its constituents, and its composition is proved in that way, it is said to be formed by synthesis.

Experiment 1.—Take a common soda-water bottle, fit it with a tight cork, then fill it with water, and invert it in the pneumatic trough. Allow hydrogen to pass into it until it is exactly two thirds full. The best way to insure this is to measure the contents of the bottle with water before the experiment, to divide this water into three portions, and to introduce these portions successively into the bottle, making marks on the outside, to correspond with the height of the water within, either with a pen and ink, or better, with slips of gummed paper. When the bottle is two thirds full of hydrogen, fill the remaining third with oxygen, which you may transfer from a bottle, in the manner described at page 30. You will understand that the bottle now contains a mixture of two parts by measure of hydrogen, with one part of oxygen. This is otherwise expressed by saying that there are two *volumes* of hydrogen to one *volume* of oxygen.

Cork the bottle tightly under water, and remove it; then wrap it all in a towel, allowing only the neck to be seen. Light a spirit-lamp, and place it on the table before you. Now hold the bottle by the towel, remove the cork, and apply the mouth of the bottle quickly to the spirit-lamp. You will get a very loud explosion, and the lamp will be blown out. Sometimes, though not very often, the bottle is broken. If this be the case it will do no harm, provided you have taken the precaution of wrapping the bottle up in a towel. Remember, once for all, never to neglect anything which I tell you to do, for you may otherwise meet with serious accidents; and never be careless or foolhardy in trying experiments, or in playing with dangerous materials. A good chemist, though brave whenever there is real occasion, should always be scrupulously careful in working, and should avoid danger whenever it is possible.

In this experiment we have another instance of intense chemical affinity.

The gases combine with a loud report, and produce water, which, if it had been possible for the bottle to be perfectly dry inside at the beginning of the experiment, would have been found in the shape of a few drops of dew moistening the inside of the glass. As it is, of course you will not see it, though it can be shown readily by suitable means.

The next experiment will serve to show that water is really produced.

Experiment 2.—Remove the wash-bottle from the hydrogen apparatus, fig. 18, take out likewise the tube *d* which led from the generator. In place of this last, you must prepare another tube.

Take a piece of glass tubing about one foot long, and exactly the same thickness as *d*. Hold it in the upper part of the spirit-lamp flame, at about four inches from one end, and turn it round and round till it begins to get soft. Then, instead of bending it as you have done before, pull it gently out till it looks like *b* in fig. 21.

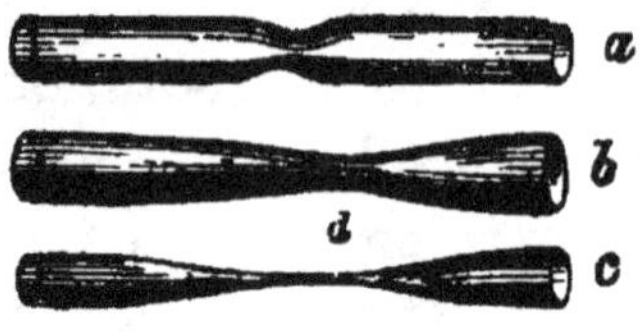

Fig. 21.

When this is the case, and while the glass is still soft, draw the two ends of the tube suddenly and quickly apart, till your hands are a foot or more asunder. The stages through which the tube passes are represented by *a*, *b*, and *c*, in fig. 21. You will thus get two pieces of tubing connected by a long, slender, and very elastic thread. This thread, wonderful as it may appear, is still a tube—it is hollow from one end to the other, and if, instead of being only a foot or two long, it had been spun out to a length of many hundred yards, which by suitable means it would be quite possible to do, every single inch of this fine thread of glass would still have been a perfect tube. When the glass is cold, cut the thread off from the longer end, with a fine file, at the point *d*. Hold this fine end for an instant in the flame, in order to soften the rough edges, and the tube will be finished. It is now called a *jet*, and is to be inserted, point upwards, in the hole from which you had taken the tube *d*, in fig. 18. It must not go to the bottom of the bottle, but only just pass through the cork. The whole arrangement is shown in fig. 22.

Fig. 22.

Prepare the hydrogen as usual in the bottle, and when the common air is completely expelled, apply a light to the jet. The gas will take fire and burn with a pale flame, which gives scarcely any light, but a great deal of heat. Now take a perfectly dry

Fig. 23.

tumbler, and hold it upside down over the flame: the sides will instantly become covered with a *dew.* This dew is the water produced by the hydrogen combining with the oxygen of the air.

This experiment is a very important as well as a very interesting one, because it draws your attention to a most important law of nature;—namely, that whenever hydrogen, or any substance containing hydrogen, is burnt in the air, water is produced. We do not generally see this water, because it passes into the air in the form of invisible vapour or gas, but its existence is none the less certain. Coals, wood, coal-gas, tallow, wax, and the numberless kinds of oil and spirit which are used for fuel, are examples of substances which contain hydrogen. Every one of these gives out in burning a greater or less quantity of water. You remember that I told you before (v. page 42) that carbonic acid was the principal product of the combustion of all sorts of fuel, so that you now see that when any of these substances are burnt, they pass into the air in the invisible forms of water and carbonic acid. When we come to the subject of air, you will find that both of these bodies are always present in it.

Experiment 3.—Take a piece of the strong German glass tubing called *combustion-tubing*, about a foot long. Into one end of it fit a cork with a short, straight tube passing through it. Connect this short tube by means of a little piece of vulcanized tubing, with the delivery-tube of the wash-bottle *e*, fig. 18. Support the other end of the long tube in some way, so that it declines a little from the end which is attached to the hydrogen apparatus. Pour out the water from the wash-bottle, and substitute for it strong sulphuric acid. This, having a strong affinity for water, will absorb it from the hydrogen, and dry the gas completely as it passes through it, before it reaches the long tube. In the long tube, at about four inches from the end nearest the apparatus, put a little *red oxide of iron*. This, which you will remember, was deposited on the sides of the jar when the watch-spring was burnt in oxygen, is the same as common red rust. The apparatus is shown in fig. 24.

Fig. 24.

When the hydrogen is passing pretty rapidly through the wash-bottle, the heat of a spirit-lamp is applied to the part of the tube where the oxide of iron is. As the latter gets hot it turns black, and drops of water are seen to collect at about *a*, and trickle down to the end of the tube. This water is produced by the hydrogen abstracting the oxygen from the oxide of iron, and consequently we find at the end of the experiment that metallic iron is left in the tube.

When no more water appears to be formed, take away the spirit-lamp and let the tube cool. Before, however, it is quite cold, take it off from the tube and cork which connect it with the rest of the apparatus, and turn the iron out through the dry end of the tube into the air. It will instantly catch fire and burn with beautiful sparks. If thrown into oxygen gas, the effect is still more striking.

Now as I have just told you that this black powder is nothing but metallic iron, you will not fail, I think, to be astonished that it should take fire so easily. It is a curious instance of the effect of fine division in promoting chemical combination.

The iron, when the oxygen is withdrawn from it, is left in such a fine and porous state, that the oxygen more readily attacks it, and they combine together so rapidly as absolutely to set the iron on fire.

Experiment 4.—You will remember (v. page 20) that when you threw potassium on water, the water was decomposed; the potassium in burning took the oxygen from the hydrogen. The hydrogen being given off in contact with flame, was again oxidized, and passed into the air as vapour of water. I will now show you a way of conducting the experiment by which we may collect the hydrogen, and in that way show that when oxygen is taken from water, hydrogen is left.

Take a test-tube four inches long and three quarters of an inch wide. Fill it with water, and invert it in a basin of water. Then take a piece of the metal sodium, dry it from the naphtha in which, like potassium, it is kept, screw it up quickly and tightly in a little piece of white blotting-paper, and, either with your fingers, or better, with a pair of crucible tongs (fig. 25), pass it up into the tube of water. As

Fig. 25.

soon as the metal touches the water, it begins to decompose it, and gas collects in the tube. When the tube is full of gas, or when no more action takes place, put your thumb under the tube, so as to close its mouth, and remove it from the water. On applying a light to the mouth of the tube, the gas burns with a pale flame. This gas is hydrogen.

The affinity of sodium for oxygen, though powerful enough to cause it to decompose water, is not quite so great as that of potassium. With potassium, flame is always the result of the decomposition, whether hot or cold water, or even ice, is used. With sodium no flame usually occurs unless the metal be thrown into hot water. Take a dinner-plate containing water nearly boiling, and throw on to it a small piece of sodium. It will take fire and burn like potassium, but with a bright-yellow flame. It is rather apt to fly about, so you had better not allow your face to be too close. After the experiment, the plate will contain a weak solution of caustic soda, or oxide of sodium.

The same experiment may be shown very prettily as follows:—

Put a little piece of blotting-paper on the surface of cold water in a tumbler, and drop on the paper a small piece of sodium. It will almost instantly inflame, and burn very quietly. The paper prevents the sodium from darting about as it usually does, and thus allows the heat to accumulate in one place.

Combining Proportions.—The preceding experiments have, I think, clearly proved that water is composed of oxygen and hydrogen; but I have as yet said nothing about the *proportions* in which the two gases combine. These are regulated by certain very important laws, which are called the *laws of combining proportion.* It is not desirable, in so small a book as the present, to go very much into the detail of these laws, especially as you will find them described at length in any of those larger books on chemistry to which this one is designed to serve as an introduction. But so important are they, that I shall, before I go any farther, try to make you understand their general nature.

When you exploded the mixture of oxygen and hydrogen in the soda-water bottle (v. page 55), you remember you took two volumes of hydrogen and only one volume of oxygen.

Now, although you thus appeared to have more hydrogen than oxygen, yet hydrogen is so much lighter than oxygen, that the one volume of oxygen weighs eight times as much as the two volumes of hydrogen. In fact, had you weighed out the gases instead of measuring them, you must have taken eight times as much oxygen by weight as hydrogen to get the right proportions in your mixture; supposing, that is, you had one ounce or one pound of hydrogen, you must have employed eight ounces or eight pounds of oxygen. If the mixture be made exactly in these proportions, the gases will combine together *entirely*, not a particle of either will be left behind; but if there be the slightest excess of either gas, it will remain after the explosion unchanged. Oxygen and hydrogen will combine together to form water, in the proportion of eight to one, and in *no other proportion*, so that nine parts of water always contain eight of oxygen and one of hydrogen.

This will enable you, with a little attention, to understand the first great law of chemical combination. It is called "The law of constant proportion," and is stated in these terms:—

1st Law.—*The same chemical compound always contains the same ingredients in the same proportion.*

In the case of water. The compound water, whether collected in England or in China, always contains the same ingredients, hydrogen and oxygen, in the same proportions,—one to eight. Water generally contains a few impurities in solution; but these of course are not part of the chemical *compound.*

This same law is true of every other chemical compound.

2nd Law.—"The law of equivalent proportions."

If you now turn to page 15, you will see that on the list of elements there, the number 8 is placed against oxygen, and the number 1 against hydrogen. Against most of the other elements other numbers are likewise placed.

You already know that eight and one are the proportions in which oxygen and hydrogen combine with one another; but this second law states another great fact about them.

The proportion in which any two bodies combine with one another, is also the proportion in which they combine with every other body. That is, that as oxygen combines with hydrogen in the proportion of eight, it will also combine with any other substance in the proportion of eight. Take the case of chlorine. Chlorine combines with hydrogen in the proportion of 35½, consequently we know by this law that it will combine with oxygen in the proportion of 35½. Accordingly we find by actual experience that 8 parts of oxygen will combine with 35½ parts of chlorine.

It is for these reasons that the numbers which are attached to the elements are called their *equivalents,* those numbers being the relative quantities by weight of the different elements which are *equivalent* to one another. You will often hear of one, two, or three equivalents of a substance. You must remember that this means, once, twice, or three times its combining proportion. Of course the numbers do not represent any absolute weight, but only proportions. Hydrogen is called one, and the others are compared with it, because hydrogen happens to be the lowest on the scale; but hydrogen might as well, though not as conveniently, have been called two, oxygen sixteen, and all the others doubled in the same way.

3rd Law.—"The law of multiple proportions."

When a body combines with another body in more than one proportion, the higher proportions are always multiples of the first or lowest.

It very frequently happens that two substances will combine together in several proportions. Let us take the case of nitrogen. Nitrogen forms no less than five distinct compounds with oxygen, every one of which has different properties. The simplest proportion in which they can combine is, of course, one equivalent of each.

Nitrogen.		Oxygen.		
1 Equivalent	= 14 .	1 Equivalent	= 8	Protoxide of Nitrogen.
1 „	= 14 .	2 „	= 16	Binoxide of Nitrogen.
1 „	= 14 .	3 „	= 24	Nitrous Acid.
1 „	= 14 .	4 „	= 32	Hyponitric Acid.
1 „	= 14 .	5 „	= 40	Nitric Acid.

The second compound contains two equivalents of oxygen; the third, three equivalents, and so on. You see by the table that the quantity of oxygen in each compound is a multiple of that in the lowest, sixteen being twice eight, twenty-four, three times eight, and so with the others. It would be easy to multiply instances of this sort; but it is unnecessary at present, because if you do not understand this one instance, you are not likely to do so from simple repetition.

4th Law.—"The law of compound proportion."

The equivalent or combining proportion of a compound, is always the sum of the equivalents of its constituents.

Thus, in the case from which we started, the equivalent of hydrogen being one, and the equivalent of oxygen eight, the equivalent of their compound water, will be the sum of these two, or nine. In the same way the equivalent of potash, which is an oxide of potassium, will be forty-seven.

Equivalent of potassium . .	39
,, oxygen . .	8
Equivalent of potash . .	47

So again with common salt, which is a compound of chlorine and sodium.

Equivalent of chlorine . .	35·5
,, sodium . .	23
Chloride of sodium . . .	58·5

Symbols.—Besides the numbers, you will see that certain letters are placed opposite to the names of the elements in the table. These are the symbols, or abbreviations, now so largely used in chemistry. In all cases they are taken from the Latin names of the elements. Thus Sn stands for Stannum, tin; Pb, for

Plumbum, lead; K, for Kalium, potassium; Na, for Natrium, sodium, and so on. Each of these symbols represents *one equivalent of the element*, and the ordinary arithmetical signs are applied to them. Thus

$$H + O, \text{ or } HO,$$

represents one equivalent of water. The second is the most usual and the most correct way of writing it, because when the sign + occurs, it generally shows either that no combination exists, or that it is a very feeble one; whereas when the two symbols are close together, it denotes that the elements or compounds are in actual union with each other, as is the case in water.

Chemical decompositions may be very conveniently represented by means of theso symbols. Thus the action of potassium on water, represented by the diagram on page 20, may be shown much more concisely in this way:—

$$HO + K = KO + H.$$

That is, potassium added to water, equals, or produces, potash and hydrogen. This way of representing decompositions by equations is now very common. Here is another instance:—

$$HgCl + KI = HgI + KCl.$$

Chloride of mercury and iodide of potassium yield iodide of mercury and chloride of potassium.

A large figure placed before a symbol, shows that all that follows it to the next + sign, or comma, or to the end of the paragraph, is to be multiplied by it. Thus—

$$2\,HgCl$$

represents two equivalents of chloride of mercury, or two equivalents of chlorine and two of mercury; but

$$Hg_2\,Cl$$

is two equivalents of mercury to one equivalent of chlorine, the small numbers only multiplying the symbol to which they are attached. Once more, $C\,O_2$ represents carbonic acid; a compound of one equivalent of carbon with two of oxygen. $2\,C\,O_2$, means two equivalents of carbonic acid, and so on. In all cases where a compound is represented, the metal, or the substance most resembling a metal, is placed first. Thus potash is written K O, and not O K.

Properties of Water.—Now that you understand, as I hope, the composition of water, it is time that you should learn something about its properties. Some of these, though very important, do not belong to the province of chemistry so much as of physics. Amongst them I may mention the subjects of expansion, convection, and conduction, with the history of steam and of latent heat, besides some others which will be found fully treated of in works on natural philosophy.

Solvent Power.—Perhaps on the whole, the most important property of water is its very great solvent power, or power of dissolving various bodies.

You know how easily sugar, salt, and alum are dissolved by it, and there are besides these bodies many hundreds of others which are with greater or less ease dissolved by water. In fact, it will dissolve more substances than any other liquid known.

Bodies differ very greatly in their degrees of solubility. Some are not dissolved at all. Others only with great difficulty, and in a large quantity of water, while some are very easily soluble, and require only a small quantity of water.

One very curious fact is, that most substances which will dissolve in water, will do so in much greater quantity in hot than in cold water, and the consequence of this is, that we can often prepare a *hot* solution, which contains more of the substance than the water will dissolve when *cold*. When this is the case, the excess deposits when the solution cools, and it generally does so, not in powder, or in irregular masses, but in beautiful geometrical figures, which are called crystals.

Crystallization.—To illustrate this, take one ounce (troy weight) of each of the following salts:—alum, sulphate of copper (blue vitriol), and bichromate of potash. Reduce them gently to powder with a mortar and pestle, and put them into three basins. On the alum pour about ten fluid ounces of water,* on the sulphate of copper, three fluid ounces, and on the bichromate of potash, seven fluid ounces. Heat them over the spirit-lamp until the salts are entirely dissolved, then place them on one side to cool. When this is the case, the bottoms of the basins will be found to be covered with small but beautiful crystals, and if a string or wire be suspended in the hot liquids, it will be encrusted with a mass of crystals.

I told you that most substances were more soluble

* Small quantities of liquids are measured by one of the graduated measures used in chemists' shops.

in hot than in cold water. Common salt and lime are exceptions to this. Salt is about equally soluble in cold and hot water, while lime is more soluble in cold than in hot water. Another important exception to this is found in those gases which are soluble in water. Instead of being more soluble in hot water, these are exactly the reverse, many of them being freely soluble in cold water, while the greater part, if not the whole, of the dissolved gas is expelled, if the solution be heated.

Impurities of Water.—Owing to the powerful solvent power which I have been speaking of, water nearly always contains a greater or less quantity of foreign substances in solution. Even rain water, which is the purest kind of natural water, is contaminated with small quantities of salts which appear to be carried up mechanically into the clouds, besides some volatile substances; but spring water, and still more sea water, contain a very considerable quantity of salts in solution, and it is to this that their *hardness* is owing. Had I space, I could tell you many interesting facts about the substances which are found dissolved in the water, the action of the soap in softening it, and other things of like importance. You must seek an explanation of them in larger books.

Distillation.—When water is heated up to a certain temperature—a temperature which is marked on the thermometer as 212°—it boils, and is gradually converted into *steam*. Steam is a colourless and invisible gas, and is not to be confounded with the white vapour which is seen to issue from the mouth of a tea-kettle.

When steam is cooled down below 212°, it *condenses*, that is, it is reconverted into water. Advantage is taken of these facts to separate water and other volatile liquids from any non-volatile impurities which they may contain, by means of a process which is called distillation. You can perform it on a small scale for yourself.

Take a small glass *retort* (*a* fig. 26), fill it about half full with water, previously coloured by a little of some non-volatile substance, such as sulphate of copper. Support the retort on the ring of a retort-stand, over a spirit-lamp, and allow its neck to dip into a flask:

Fig. 26.

this flask is called a *receiver*. When the water boils, it passes over as steam, and is again condensed in the receiver. By allowing this process to go on, the whole of the water will be obtained quite pure and colourless, in the receiver. It is better not to allow the process to go on till the retort is dry, as the heat is then apt to break the glass. When this process is conducted on a large scale, as in the manufacture of spirits, large copper retorts are used, which are then called *stills*.

Filtration.—Besides the chemical impurities, as the substances dissolved in the water are called, water, as well as other liquids, frequently contains mechanical impurities—things, that is, which are not dissolved in the water, but are merely floating suspended in it. It is not necessary to have recourse to distillation to separate these; they can be removed just as well by *filtration.* Take a square of white blotting-paper, or filter-paper as it is called, fold it in half, then in half again, and cut the corners off, so as to make the paper round (*a*, fig. 27). Open it in the

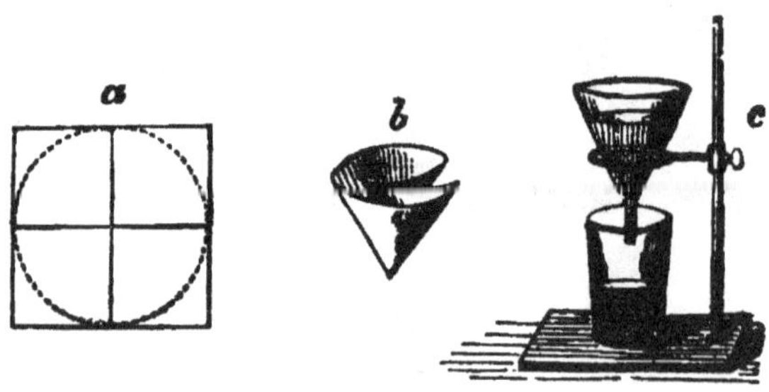

Fig. 27.

way shown in *b*, and place it in a funnel rather larger than itself. Moisten it with distilled water, and place a tumbler under it. Then mix in another vessel a little water, with some cinder-ashes, or some other impurity. Pour this dirty water carefully on to the paper filter, and you will find that clear water will pass through, the impurities being all retained by the filter. Of course the filter will not prevent things *dissolved* in water from passing.

Compounds of Water.—Water forms definite compounds with a large number of bodies. It unites with many acids, and is then regarded as a base (v. page 86). It also unites with many bases, and then appears to play the part of an acid (v. page 142).

Besides these combinations, water enters into the composition of a large number of crystallized salts, and in these cases the crystalline form seems to depend upon its presence. For this cause it is distinguished as " water of crystallization."

Common alum affords an instance of this (v. page 111).

Many of the salts described in the following pages, contain water when crystallized; this water may be expelled from them by heat. I have usually omitted it, in order to render the formulæ of the salts simpler.

Binoxide of Hydrogen. $H\,O_2$.

Water is not the only oxide of hydrogen. By a very difficult process, a second may be obtained, which has some remarkable properties. It is a colourless, transparent, and somewhat oil-like liquid, soluble in water and acids. A very slight elevation of temperature converts it into water and oxygen.

CHAPTER VI.

NITROGEN.

N = 14.

Preparation.—I HAVE already told you that common air is a mixture of oxygen and nitrogen. This being the case, it is evident that all we have to do to prepare nitrogen, is to remove the oxygen from common air, when the nitrogen will be left behind. There are many ways of effecting this, but the simplest is as follows:—

Take a basin full of water. Place a little basin, an inch or two across, so that it may float on the surface of the water in the large basin. Put into this little basin a piece of phosphorus about the size of a pea, light the phosphorus, and immediately invert over it, with the open end touching the water, a large gas-jar. The phosphorus in burning will absorb all the oxygen from the air in the jar, and will unite with it to form phosphoric acid. When the phosphorus goes out for want of more oxygen to support its combustion, you must still leave the jar in contact with the water for some time, until the white fumes which at first fill it disappear. They consist of phosphoric acid, and this is very soluble in water, so that after a time it is entirely dissolved by the water. When this is the case, shake the jar until the little basin fills with water and falls to the bottom; the jar of nitrogen may then be removed by a plate in the usual manner.

Properties.—The properties of nitrogen are entirely and curiously negative. It is not combustible. It does

Fig. 28.

not support combustion. It is not poisonous, but it will not support life; it has no taste, no smell, and is not visible; and, with a few unimportant exceptions, it will not combine directly with any other element. And yet this apparently inert body, when in combination, produces some of the most active and powerful compounds with which we are acquainted.

There are no very striking experiments to be done with nitrogen. Plunge a taper into a jar of the gas: you will observe that it is at once extinguished, without igniting the gas.

Before describing the compounds of nitrogen, I have a little more to say about the air.

THE AIR.

If you noticed the jar at the conclusion of the experiment by which you made nitrogen, you saw that the water had risen in it until it occupied about one fifth of the whole jar. This part corresponds with the quantity of oxygen absorbed by the phosphorus, so that you see about one fifth of the whole volume of the air is oxygen. More exactly, the proportion of the two gases is as follows :—

	By Weight.	By Volume.
Oxygen	23	21
Nitrogen	77	79
	100	100

I have already told you (v. page 18) that the two gases are not combined together, but only mixed; and, in speaking of combustion, I have explained that the principal use of the nitrogen is to dilute and modify the action of the oxygen. Besides these two gases, the atmosphere always contains other gases, the most important of which are carbonic acid, and the vapour of water. You remember that animals in breathing, as well as fuel of all kinds in burning, give out carbonic acid to the air. Besides this, it is found issuing from the ground in some parts of the earth; all putrefying organic matters evolve it, and many volcanoes give out vast quantities of it. How is it then that it does not increase in amount?—that it does not collect in such quantities as to become dangerous, since we know it to be a very poisonous gas? The reason of all this is, that by a very wonderful provision of Nature, plants breathe and absorb this same gas which is so poisonous to man.

Man and other animals, you remember, draw oxygen into their lungs, and breathe out carbonic acid. Plants of all kinds, on the contrary, absorb carbonic acid, and give out oxygen through their leaves, which are supposed to answer to the lungs of animals.

The quantity of water which can exist in the shape of vapour, either in air or in an empty space, depends entirely on the temperature. The higher this is, the more water will generally be found in the air as vapour, so that it often happens that when the air is suddenly cooled, there is more water than can remain as vapour in it. When this takes place high up in the air, the excess of water falls as rain, snow, or hail, according to the temperature. When the air is cooled on the surface of the ground, dew, or hoar-frost is deposited.

It is to this tendency of liquids to assume the form of vapour that we owe the ready drying up of water which has been spilt. But for this it would be almost impossible to dry either our skins or anything else which had once become wet.

Oxides of Nitrogen.

The following is a list of the compounds which nitrogen forms with oxygen :—

	Symbol.		Equivalent.
Protoxide of Nitrogen . .	NO	=	22
Binoxide of Nitrogen . . .	NO_2	=	30
Nitrous Acid	NO_3	=	38
Hyponitric Acid . . .	NO_4	=	46
Nitric Acid	NO_5	=	54

You will observe that the lowest of these oxides is called "protoxide," and the next "binoxide." These are terms very commonly used. They are derived from two words, signifying first and second, because they are the first and second oxides of nitrogen. The other three oxides are acids (see page 44), and you may remark that their names are likewise modified to prevent their being confounded with one another.

I do not propose to describe all these oxides, but shall content myself with noticing the first and the last, as being two of the most interesting.

Protoxide of Nitrogen, or laughing-gas, NO.—This gas, which is well known from the peculiar properties from which it derives one of its titles, may be obtained by heating the salt called nitrate of ammonia, in the same apparatus as that in which oxygen was prepared (v. page 28). The pneumatic trough, as well as the bottles to be filled, must be filled with warm water, as the gas is absorbed by cold.

The decomposition of the salt may be represented by the following formula:—

$$NH_4O, NO_5 = 2NO + 4HO.$$

NH_4O is ammonia, a compound consisting of one equivalent of nitrogen, four of hydrogen, and one of oxygen. NO_5 is nitric acid, which, combined with the ammonia, forms nitrate of ammonia. When this is heated, it is decomposed into two equivalents of protoxide of nitrogen, and four of water.

Properties.—Protoxide of nitrogen is a powerful supporter of combustion. All the things which burn in oxygen, will burn, though not so brightly, in this gas. You may try a taper, a piece of charcoal, a fragment of phosphorus, &c. It is very heavy, and has a faint though agreeable smell. But by far its most curious property is the one to which I have before alluded, namely, its peculiar and intoxicating effect on the human body. When it is quite pure, it may be safely breathed for a short time, and though its effects are now and then unpleasant, if not dangerous, yet generally it produces the most delightful and exhilarating sensations. Sometimes, too, it has a most ludicrous effect on the person who inhales it. I have seen a man stand bobbing up and down, with his arms and legs bent, his fingers holding his nose, and his body inclined forward, and utterly without the power of controlling his own emotions. Sometimes the natural character of the individual is brought more clearly out. One man will show the strongest disposition in the world to fight, and will attack every one in his neighbourhood; another will dance, another will do nothing but laugh in the most absurd and idiotic way. One very curious thing about it is, that in most cases no depression or languor follows the fit of excitement, as is the case with common intoxication; but, on the contrary, the patient generally appears in better spirits for the rest of the day. This remarkable property of protoxide of nitrogen was first observed by Sir Humphry Davy.

Nitric Acid, $N\,O_5$.—This acid, which is commonly known as aqua-fortis, can be prepared very conveniently from nitrate of potash, or common nitre.

Take a *tubulated retort*,* put into it about four ounces of powdered nitre, and pour on the nitre, by means of a funnel placed in the stoppered neck of the retort,

* A plain retort may be made to answer the purpose, if the sulphuric acid be poured carefully in through a thistle-headed funnel.

about an equal quantity of sulphuric acid. Stir the two together with a glass rod, taking care not to crack the retort; replace the stopper, and arrange the retort on a retort-stand, with its mouth dipping into a flask, or receiver, in the manner shown in fig. 29.

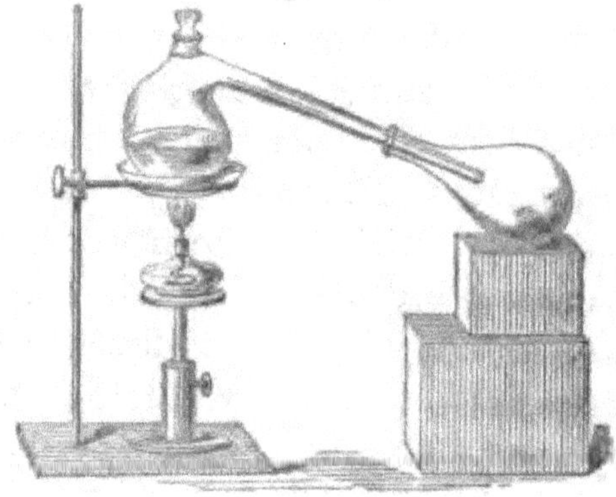

Fig. 29.

The retort had better rest on a little iron basin containing sand. This is called a sand-bath, and is very often used when we wish to apply heat in a gentle and gradual manner.

The heat of a spirit-lamp is now to be applied to the sand-bath. As the temperature rises, fumes of nitric acid rise in the retort, distil over, and are condensed in the receiver, which had better be kept cool by means of a wet rag wrapped round it. When about half a fluid ounce has collected in the receiver, the operation must be stopped, as otherwise the retort is rather apt to break. You will not have enough acid for the experiments you are going to try, but this does not matter, for it is very cheap.

It is now made on a very large scale, many tons of the material being employed in the manufacture.

Properties.—Nitric acid is one of the most powerful acids with which we are acquainted. A great many of the metals are dissolved, or otherwise acted on by it, and many organic substances—that is, substances which derive their origin from either the animal or vegetable kingdom—are likewise affected by it. We will illustrate this before we go any farther.

Experiment 1.—Take a piece of silk, either white or unbleached, as it is generally imported. Pour on this a few drops of nitric acid. In a few moments wash the silk in a little water, or the texture will be entirely destroyed by the acid. When it is dry you will find that where the acid has been in contact with it a yellow stain has been produced. This is likewise the case if quill pens are immersed for a few minutes in the acid, and then washed. If by accident your fingers become touched with it during any of these experiments, you must be careful to wash it off immediately, as when it remains for any time on the skin, it destroys it, and sometimes produces painful sores. Even if it be very soon washed off, it usually leaves the skin of a bright yellow colour.

Experiment 2.—Now try its effect on oil of turpentine.

Take a small wide-mouthed bottle, one like pomatum is sold in will do, tie it across the end of a stick three or four feet long, and put into it a little nitric acid, and about half the quantity of sulphuric acid. Warm a common dinner-plate before the fire till you can only just bear your hand to it, and place it in some convenient place out of doors, where the thick smoke which is produced will not inconvenience you. Pour on the hot plate just about enough turpentine to cover the bottom, and, holding the bottle with the acid in it at arm's length with the rod, pour the acid quickly on the turpentine. A sudden and very intense blaze of light will be produced, the turpentine will be consumed, and dense black smoke will ascend into the air.

Experiment 3.—Sprinkle a little powdered indigo on a plate, and pour on it a little nitric acid. The blue colour will be changed into a yellow. Another more striking way of performing this experiment is to dye a piece of calico with a solution of indigo in sulphuric acid, and to apply the nitric acid in drops to it. Wherever the acid touches, the blue colour is changed to yellow, and this is the way that the yellow spots on silk handkerchiefs are produced.

Nitric acid produces most curious and important alterations in many other organic substances.

When cotton wool is treated with it, the curious substance called gun-cotton is produced. In appearance, this substance is just like ordinary cotton, but instead of burning like cotton, it ignites with the slightest spark, and disappears instantly, with a bright flash. When it is well prepared, it is entirely consumed in burning, and leaves no trace of ash behind. The result of this is, that a piece of it may safely be burnt on the hand, or even resting on a plateful of gunpowder. The hand is not scorched, and the gunpowder is scarcely ever inflamed.

Experiment 4.—Nitric acid, as I have already told you, has a powerful effect on many metals. Put a few shreds of copper, or "copper-turnings," into a glass, and having added a very little water to them, pour on them some nitric acid. In a few minutes the copper will begin to dissolve, red fumes will be given off, and a beautiful blue solution will be left in the place of the copper. This blue solution is called *nitrate of copper*, though it might more correctly be called *nitrate of the oxide of copper*.

Experiment 5.—Instead of the copper, use a globule of metallic mercury, or quicksilver.

In this case you will get a colourless solution, though the red fumes will be given off as before. The colourless solution contains the *nitrate of mercury*.

Oxy-Acids.

Nitric acid combines with a great many bases, or oxides of metals (v. page 23), producing with them salts which are called nitrates. In speaking of the compounds which oxygen forms with other elements (page 44), I told you that a large class of them were acids. These acids are called oxygen acids, or *oxy-acids*, from the fact of their being oxides. Nitric acid is one of them. Now these oxygen acids can never combine with a metal; they must always have the oxide of the metal produced before they can combine with it to form a salt.

You might naturally say, on reading this, "Well, but did I not pour nitric acid on the metal copper, not on the oxide, and did I not then get a nitrate of copper?" Not in reality. The process, which appeared all one, was really two distinct processes. Nitric acid is very easily decomposed, and when it is, it generally yields a portion of the oxygen which it contains to whatever is nearest to it. In the case before us, the copper is oxidized at the expense of a portion of the nitric acid.

This is the first stage of the proceedings. As fast as the oxide of copper is formed, it is dissolved up by another portion of nitric acid, and the blue salt called nitrate of copper is produced.

This is the second stage.

The first is represented in symbols thus:—

$$3\,Cu + HO,NO_5 = 3\,CuO + HO + NO_2.$$

That is, three equivalents of copper, and one of nitric acid (besides one of water, which I shall explain presently), produce three of oxide of copper, one of water, and one of *binoxide of nitrogen* (v. page 77). This binoxide of nitrogen is a colourless gas; but when it comes in contact with the air, it absorbs two equivalents of oxygen, and is converted into *hyponitric acid*, which constitutes the red fumes that pass off during the experiment:—

$$NO_2 + 2\,O \text{ (from the air)} = NO_4.$$

If you were to dissolve pure *oxide of* copper in nitric acid, the same blue solution would be produced as in this case, but no red fumes would arise. The process, as well as the second stage of the one before us, may be represented thus:—

$$CuO + HO,NO_5 = CuO,NO_5 + HO.$$

I have spoken of this experiment as consisting of two stages, in order to make the matter simpler to you, but in reality both processes go on, very probably, at the same time. The whole affair may be thus shown :—

$$3\ Cu+4\ (H\ O,\ N\ O_5)=3\ (Cu\ O,\ N\ O_5)+4\ H\ O+N\ O_2.$$

The mercury experiment is somewhat similar. From the ease with which nitric acid parts with its oxygen, it is called a powerful *oxidizing agent.*

Remember for the future, that all oxygen acids combine only with the oxides of metals. The salts which are produced in this way are called "*oxygen salts,*" or "*oxy-salts.*"

In all the formulæ in which I have introduced nitric acid, you will have seen that water (H O) is included. The fact is, that nitric acid, as well as all other oxygen acids, requires water to be combined with it before it can be regarded as a true acid. Anhydrous nitric acid, that is, nitric acid free from water, or $N\ O_5$, has only been obtained within the last few years, and then by a difficult process; and even when it is obtained it is not considered as possessing acid properties until it is combined with water. The strongest nitric acid contains one equivalent of water, or $H\ O,\ N\ O_5$. This is called "fuming nitric acid." The acid which you have employed, and which is the more common, consists of $4\ H\ O,\ N\ O_5$. In the formulæ which I have given, I have spoken of the acid, for convenience, as $H\ O,\ N\ O_5$. *Remember that all oxygen acids require water to be combined with them before they will possess acid properties.*

The water is really combined with them; they are not merely dissolved in it; and we may therefore regard hydrated nitric acid as *nitrate of water*, and suppose that when a base unites with it, the base only takes the place of the weaker base, water :—.

$$HONO_5 + KO = KO, NO_5 + HO.$$

I think this will be the best place to explain the process by which hydrogen is made. I deferred it until you had learned something about the action of acids on metals. The following is the formula of the process:—

$$Zn + HO, SO_3 = ZnO, SO_3 + H.$$

The zinc is oxidized at the expense of the water of the sulphuric acid. The oxide of zinc (Zn O) so produced combines with the sulphuric acid, forming sulphate of the oxide of zinc, or sulphate of zinc (Zn O, S O_3), while the hydrogen of the water is set free.

The object of using so much more water than is here represented is to dissolve the sulphate of zinc which forms in the generator, and which would otherwise form a coating over the zinc, and prevent the further action of the acid.

A little attention will make the whole process quite plain to you.

Ammonia, NH_3.

This important gas may be prepared by mixing together, in a Florence or other flask, about equal weights of quick-lime and the salt called hydrochlorate of ammonia, or chloride of ammonium, both in powder, and heating the flask gently on a sand-bath. The gas is very soluble in water, but as it is lighter than air, it may be collected by displacement, like hydrogen (v. page 49):—

$$N\,H_3,\,H\,Cl + Ca\,O = Ca\,Cl + H\,O + N\,H_3.$$

Properties.—The most important property of ammonia gas is, that when it combines with water it produces the powerful base known as liquid ammonia, or, for shortness, ammonia, $N\,H_3,\,H\,O$. This is now generally regarded, not as a hydrate of ammonia gas, a compound, that is, of $N\,H_3$ with $H\,O$, but as the oxide of a compound metal *ammonium*. It is only a question of how the equivalents are to be arranged; but that is a very difficult one to decide. You will see by the following symbols that the number of equivalents is the same in both cases:—

$$\underset{\text{Hydrate of Ammonia.}}{N\,H_3,\,H\,O} = \underset{\text{Oxide of Ammonium.}}{N\,H_4\,O.}$$

This compound metal has never been obtained, so that it is entirely *hypothetical;* but a compound of it with mercury has been discovered which renders its existence probable. According to this view, the decomposition in preparing ammonia would be as follows:—

$$\underset{\text{Chloride of Ammonium.}}{N\,H_4\,Cl} + \underset{\text{Lime.}}{Ca\,O} = \underset{\text{Chloride of Calcium.}}{Ca\,Cl} + \underset{\text{Water.}}{H\,O} + \underset{\text{Ammonia.}}{N\,H_3.}$$

In the former case the salt employed would be called hydrochlorate of ammonia, and in the present, chloride of ammonium. This salt is the one which was produced when hydrochloric acid and ammonia gases were mixed (page 19) :—

$$N H_3 + H Cl = N H_4 Cl.$$

To show the solubility of the gas, remove the stopper from a bottle of it, and instantly invert it in a basin of water. The water will rush up, especially if the bottle be shaken, and very nearly fill it. If the water be previously coloured with a little tincture of litmus, reddened with some acid, another important fact will be proved by the experiment, namely, that a *base* is produced. The red litmus will be turned back to blue. Ammonia can always be detected by its powerful smell, which is that to which smelling-salts and hartshorn owe their pungency. Solution of ammonia, potash, and soda are the three *alkalies*, of which such frequent mention is made. I give the symbols for all three, that you may see that they are oxides of metals, though one of these metals is a compound, and the other two, elements :—

$N H_4 O$. Ammonia.
$K O$. Potash.
$Na O$. Soda.

CHAPTER VII.

CHLORINE, IODINE, BROMINE, FLUORINE.

CHLORINE, Cl = 35·5.

Preparation.—THIS gas is best prepared in the following manner. Take a flask (*a*, fig. 30), fit it with an acid funnel and bent tube. Then put into it some powdered binoxide of manganese; pour through the funnel

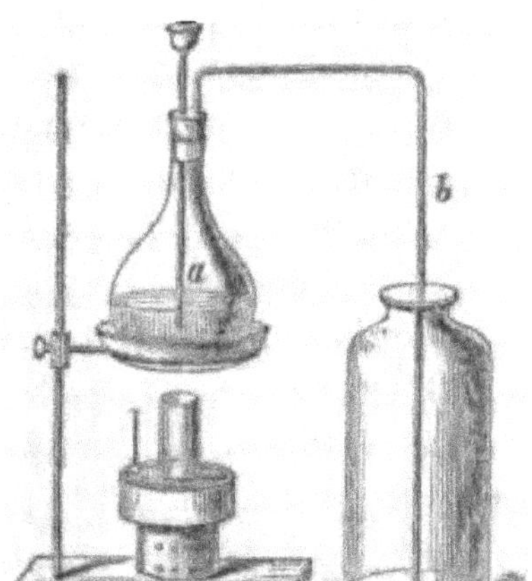

Fig. 30.

rather more than enough hydrochloric acid to cover it. Apply the heat of a sand-bath to the flask, and a greenish-yellow gas will soon be given off in considerable quantity. This is the chlorine.

It is best collected by displacement, only that in this case, as the gas is heavier than air, the bottle must stand mouth-upwards, and the tube pass down to its bottom. You will understand the arrangement by examining the annexed cut (fig. 30).

It is easy in this case to tell when the bottle is full, on account of the colour of the gas.

The explanation of this process is this:—

$$Mn\,O_2 + 2\,H\,Cl = Mn\,Cl + 2\,H\,O + Cl.$$

One equivalent of binoxide of manganese, and two of hydrochloric acid, yield one equivalent of chloride of manganese, two of water, and one of chlorine.

Properties.—Chlorine gas is a greenish-yellow, and very heavy gas. It is very poisonous, and produces, when even a small quantity of it is breathed, a most painful and irritating cough. Almost the first time I made it, as a boy, I was clumsy enough to get some of it down my throat, and in consequence had an attack of inflammation of the lungs, which was very nearly bringing my chemistry to an untimely end. I hope you will take better care; if you do, you need not be in the least afraid, especially if you take the precaution to place the apparatus under a chimney, or in some other place where any gas which may escape can do no harm. If you should get a little into your throat, take a lump of sugar, moistened with a little very dilute ammonia, and inhale some of the vapour from smelling-salts, or hartshorn. The ammonia will combine with the chlorine, and *neutralize* it. Chlorine is incombustible, but it supports powerfully the combustion of other bodies.

Experiment 1.—Plunge a lighted taper into a bottle of the gas. It will continue to burn, but with a very dim and smoky flame.

Experiment 2.—Put a little piece of phosphorus into a deflagrating spoon (page 37), and dip it into the gas without previously lighting it, as you remember was necessary in the case of oxygen. It will immediately take fire and burn, though with a pale flame, very different from the magnificent light produced in oxygen. *Chloride of phosphorus* is produced.

Experiment 3.—The thin leaf-copper called "Dutch Gold" can be bought for about twopence a book. Take a leaf of this up with a glass rod, by breathing against the rod, and then touching the leaf with it. Dip the rod with the Dutch gold on the end of it into a bottle of chlorine; it will take fire and burn with a red smoky flame, producing *chloride of copper*.

Experiment 4.—A little of the metal called antimony, reduced to powder (it is very brittle), and sprinkled into a bottle of the gas, likewise inflames, and gives a shower of white sparks.

Experiment 5.—Dip a piece of white blotting-paper into oil of turpentine, and then attach it to the end of a glass rod, and immerse it in chlorine. It gives a thick smoke, and sometimes inflames, especially if shaken in the gas. Chlorine is soluble in water, and its solution possesses some remarkable properties. Allow the delivery-tube in fig. 30 to pass to the bottom of a bottle containing water; the water absorbs a portion of the gas, and gradually assumes a yellow colour.

Experiment 6.—*Bleaching power of Chlorine.*—Chlorine

is of the most immense importance in the present day, from its very powerful bleaching properties. These you can illustrate in the following manner:—Take three glasses, fill them respectively two-thirds full with very weak decoctions of litmus, brazil-wood, and turmeric, producing thus, blue, pink, and yellow solutions. Pour a little chlorine-water into each of them, and stir them; the colours of all three will be almost instantly destroyed.

Oxides of Chlorine.

	Symbol.	Equivalent.
Hypochlorous Acid	$Cl\,O$ =	43·5
Chlorous Acid	$Cl\,O_3$ =	59·5
Peroxide of Chlorine	$Cl\,O_4$ =	67·5
Chloric Acid	$Cl\,O_5$ =	75·5
Perchloric Acid	$Cl\,O_7$ =	91·5

These compounds are all very difficult, and one or two very dangerous to make. Hypochlorous acid forms with lime the salt called hypochlorite of lime ($Ca\,O, Cl\,O$), which, by some, is supposed to constitute the active part of common *chloride* of lime.

Chloric acid is chiefly interesting from its entering into the composition of *chlorate of potash* ($K\,O, Cl\,O_5$). You have already met with that salt in the preparation of oxygen (page 28), and you will now understand the reason that it is used. When it is heated, it parts with the whole of the oxygen which it contains, and *chloride of potassium* is left behind:—

$$K\,O, Cl\,O_5 = K\,Cl + 6\,O.$$

The binoxide of manganese is not changed during

the process, and its use appears to be merely mechanical. Chlorate of potash forms an essential part of many explosive mixtures. Lucifer matches, and the composition called "percussion powder," both contain it. I will describe one or two experiments with the salt; but must caution you in the first place not to use more of the materials than I advise, as otherwise the experiments might become dangerous.

Experiment 1.—Take about as much as will lie on a sixpence, of powdered chlorate of potash and an equal quantity of *lump sugar*, previously powdered *separately* from the chlorate of potash. Mix them together with a piece of card on a sheet of paper. Then put this mixture on a brick, and just touch the powder with a glass rod dipped into strong sulphuric acid; a bright flash of blue light will be produced.

Experiment 2.—Put about a grain of chlorate of potash into a perfectly dry and warm mortar, with about an equal quantity of flowers of sulphur; rub the mixture forcibly with the pestle, and a succession of sharp cracks, accompanied by little flashes of light, will be observed.

Experiment 3.—Take a grain of the salt, and half a grain of phosphorus, wrap them up in a scrap of paper, put it on a stone, and strike it with a hammer. A loud detonation or explosion follows.

Experiment 4.—Dip a piece of cotton cloth into a strong solution of this salt, and dry it thoroughly. If a piece of this cloth be put into a warm mortar, and rubbed with the pestle, a number of small explosions will be heard, and very often the cloth will take fire. The same cloth is also inflamed by pouring on it a few drops of strong sulphuric acid.

Hydrochloric Acid, H Cl.

This important gas may be procured by heating together a mixture of common salt and sulphuric acid. The same apparatus which was used for chlorine (fig. 30) may be employed, and the gas collected in the same way:—

$$Na\,Cl + H\,O, S\,O_3 = Na\,O, S\,O_3 + H\,Cl.$$

Common salt is the *chloride of sodium*, and yields its chlorine to the hydrogen of the water which is combined with the sulphuric acid. Sulphate of soda ($Na\,O, S\,O_3$) is left in the flask.*

Properties.—Hydrochloric acid is a colourless and very heavy gas, which fumes strongly in the air. It is very soluble in water, as you can prove by inverting a bottle of it in water, in the same manner as you did with ammonia. The water in this case, however, should be coloured with *blue* litmus, which will be changed to red, showing the presence of an acid.

Hydrochloric acid dissolves a good many metals and metallic oxides. You can try this for yourself with zinc and iron among the former, and with potash, lime, red oxide of mercury, and the oxides of nickel and cobalt among the latter. In all these cases a

* When excess of sulphuric acid is used, the salt left in the retort is bisulphate of soda.

$$Na\,Cl + 2(H\,O, S\,O_3) = Na\,O, H\,O, 2\,S\,O_3 + H\,Cl.$$

These are the proportions of acid and salt which it is best to use.

chloride of the metal is produced, and here it is necessary that I should say a few words on the nature of these salts.

Hydracids.

Under the head of nitric acid I have told you that the large class of oxygen acids to which that body belongs, never combine with metals, but only with the oxides of metals. Now hydrochloric acid is the representative of a not very large, but very important class of acids, which do not contain any oxygen, but are composed of a non-metallic element, combined with *hydrogen*. They are called *hydrogen* acids, or *hydracids*, and are always distinguished by the prefix "hydro." Here are a few examples:—

H Cl . . . . Hydrochloric acid.
H S . . . . Hydrosulphuric acid.
H I . . . . Hydriodic acid.
H Br . . . . Hydrobromic acid.

When one of these acids dissolves a metal, the *halogen*, that is the second element in it, combines with the metal, and hydrogen is set free. Thus with zinc:—

$$Zn + H\,Cl = Zn\,Cl + H.$$

The chlorine combines with the zinc, forming chloride of zinc, and the hydrogen is liberated. When the acid dissolves the oxide of a metal, the hydrogen leaves the acid and combines with the oxygen of the base, forming water, while a chloride of the metal is produced, as before :—

$$Zn\,O + H\,Cl = Zn\,Cl + H\,O.$$

These salts, such as chloride of zinc, iodide of potassium, and the like, are called *haloid salts*, from the Greek word *halos*, the sea, because sea salt, or chloride of sodium, is one of them. You must remember that a true haloid salt never contains oxygen. I will give you one more example of the formation of one of these salts to impress the theory on your minds :—

$$Fe_2\,O_3 + 3\,H\,Cl = Fe_2\,Cl_3 + 3\,H\,O;$$

that is, one equivalent of sesquioxide of iron, with three equivalents of hydrochloric acid, yield one of sesquichloride of iron, and three of water.

In obtaining oxygen from chlorate of potash, we convert an oxy-salt into a haloid salt,—chlorate of potash into chloride of potassium :—

$$K\,O, Cl\,O_5 = K\,Cl + 6\,O.$$

Tests for Hydrochloric Acid.—We possess two very valuable tests for the presence of this acid.

1. If the acid be free, that is, if it be not combined with any base, it may be detected by the white fumes which its vapour gives with the vapour of ammonia (page 19). Put a little dilute hydrochloric acid into a test-tube, and dip into the tube, without, however, touching the acid, a glass rod moistened with ammonia. The white fumes, which consist of chloride of ammonium, will immediately appear, and fill the tube :—

$$H\,Cl + N\,H_3 = N\,H_4\,Cl.$$

2. Hydrochloric acid, whether free or in combination, can always be detected by *nitrate of silver.* Take a little solution of any chloride—the chloride of sodium (common salt) will do very well—and add to it a little solution of nitrate of silver. A white curdy precipitate will instantly form in the clear solution, consisting of chloride of silver :—

Chloride of Sodium.		Nitrate of Silver.		Chloride of Silver.		Nitrate of Soda.
$NaCl$	+	AgO, NO_5	=	$AgCl$	+	NaO, NO_5.

If this precipitate be treated with nitric acid, it will be found to be quite insoluble, but if ammonia be added instead, it will soon dissolve. Chloride of silver blackens when exposed to the sun's light.

IODINE, I = 127.

This element is generally procured from kelp, which is a name given to the ashes of seaweed. It is usually found in flat black crystalline plates, which have a metallic lustre, although iodine is not a metal. It is volatile, and its vapour has a most splendid violet or purple colour. You may prove this by putting a few grains of iodine into a dry flask and heating it over a lamp. In a few minutes the flask will be filled with the beautiful vapour I have spoken of. As the flask cools, this will be deposited on the sides of the glass in the form of small crystals. Iodine is slightly soluble in water. Iodine forms several compounds with oxygen, the most important of which is iodic acid, IO_5

With hydrogen it forms the hydracid, hydriodic acid, which gives rise to the salts called *iodides*.

Test for Iodine.—Iodine when free, forms a beautiful blue compound with common starch; when the iodine is in combination, this colour is not produced. Mix a little solution of starch with a solution of iodide of potassium. The mixture will remain colourless. But if a drop of chlorine water, or nitric acid, be poured into it, the blue colour will immediately be produced. The reason of this is, that the chlorine takes the potassium from the iodine, and leaves the latter free :—

$$KI + Cl = KCl + I.$$

BROMINE, Br = 80.

This is a red, poisonous liquid, which gives out a most disagreeable and suffocating vapour. It is intermediate in its properties between chlorine and iodine. Like the latter, it is found in sea water.

FLUORINE, F = 19.

Though this is always reckoned as an element, and though there can be no doubt that it exists, yet it has never as yet been fairly separated from its combinations. It has the most powerful affinity for the metals, and hence it is that it is so difficult to confine it, for no sooner do we free it from one combination than it enters into another. It is found in the mineral called fluor spar, which is a fluoride of calcium.

Hydrofluoric Acid, HF.—This acid is chiefly characterized by its powerful action on glass. This it corrodes and dissolves with wonderful energy, and for this reason it is often used for etching on glass. To effect this, the glass is coated over with wax, and the desired pattern drawn with a point, through the wax. The glass is then covered with hydrofluoric acid, which corrodes wherever the wax has been scratched away.

CHAPTER VIII.

SULPHUR, PHOSPHORUS, SELENIUM.

SULPHUR, S = 16.

This element is found in great abundance; sometimes native, that is in an uncombined condition, but more often combined with iron or some other element. It is most usually met with at shops in two shapes, viz., roll-sulphur, or brimstone, and flowers of sulphur.

Properties.—Sulphur is, as you well know, a yellow solid. When it is heated above a certain point (232°) it melts, and if the heat be raised much above this, it assumes a peculiar glue-like appearance, and a very dark colour. If it be now poured into cold water, it retains the dark colour and tough and elastic consistence for some time, and while it is in this state it may be used to take impressions from seals, medals, &c. After some hours the original yellow colour and brittle character will return, but the marks made on it during its *plastic* condition, as it is called, will remain. Sulphur boils at a temperature of about 792°, and becomes converted into a vapour. When this vapour is condensed, the sulphur is re-deposited in the form of powder. This powder is what is usually called "flowers of sulphur." You see that this process is the same with solids, as distillation with liquids. In this case it is not called distillation, but *sublimation*. Sulphur is capable of crystallizing very beautifully. Melt some in a Florence flask, and allow it to cool until a crust is formed on the sur face. Break a small hole in this crust with a wire, and pour out the still liquid portion through the hole. When the sulphur is quite cold, break the flask off from the mass, and saw the latter in two, or take the crust carefully off. The inside will be found full of the most beautiful, needle-like crystals.

Oxides of Sulphur.

Sulphur forms no less than seven distinct compounds with oxygen, but only two of these are of sufficient importance to merit description here.

Sulphurous Acid, SO_2.—This, as I told you under oxygen, is the invariable product when sulphur is burnt either in the air or in oxygen. It may be prepared by heating together in a flask, copper turnings and sulphuric acid. A portion of the oxygen from the latter is employed in oxidizing the copper :—

$$Cu + 2\,H\,O,\,S\,O_3 = Cu\,O,\,S\,O_3 + 2\,H\,O + S\,O_2.$$

Sulphate of copper ($CuO,\ S\,O_3$) remains as a blue solution. The gas may be collected by displacement, exactly like chlorine.

Properties.—Sulphurous acid is a colourless gas, very heavy, and soluble in cold water. It is a non-supporter of combustion, is very poisonous, and has the peculiar smell with which we are all so familiar in burning sulphur. It is likewise a useful bleaching agent, as you may prove by dipping into a bottle of the gas, a piece of litmus paper, previously moistened. The paper is first turned red by the acid, and then slowly bleached.

Sulphuric Acid, $S\,O_3$.—By far the most important oxide of sulphur is the one which is called *sulphuric acid*. It is prepared in immense quantities by a process which is too complicated for you to understand at present, but which mainly depends on the oxidation of sulphurous acid. Oblong leaden chambers are used in the manufacture, and these are made of the most gigantic size, it being no uncommon thing for them to be more than a hundred feet in length. One eminent London firm employs two platinum stills for concentrating the acid, one of which cost 1500*l*., and the other 2000*l*.

Properties.—Anhydrous sulphuric acid, or $S\,O_3$, is difficult and rather dangerous to prepare. It is a white crystalline solid. The sulphuric acid, or "oil of vitriol," as it is sometimes called, which is sold in the shops, is a compound of the dry acid with one equivalent of water, $H\,O, S\,O_3$. Unless it is bought as pure, it is almost sure to contain lead and other impurities.

You are already familiar with some of the most important properties of this powerful acid. It blackens and destroys nearly all organic substances, setting free the carbon they contain. This you saw in the case of sugar (v. page 12). It has an energetic action on some salts, as chlorate of potash (page 93), and has a powerful affinity for water. If you pour into a beaker some sulphuric acid, and then add to it twice its bulk of cold water, the mixture will become so hot that you cannot bear your hand to the outside. Dip into it a test-tube containing a little water. In a few minutes the water will boil. Another curious experiment, is to trace any words or design you like on a linen cloth with dilute sulphuric acid, and then hold it before the fire. The parts which were moistened with the sulphuric acid will gradually become black, though before they were not visible. This is because the heat drives a portion of the water off from the acid, and it consequently becomes sufficiently concentrated to destroy the texture of the fabric.

Sulphuric acid forms with bases a large class of salts, which are called *sulphates*. Sulphate of magnesia (Epsom salts), sulphate of soda (Glauber's salts), and sulphate of iron (copperas, or green vitriol), are examples of them.

Hydrosulphuric Acid, H S.

Into the generator of the apparatus in which you made hydrogen (fig. 18), put some small pieces of *sulphide of iron*. Fill the bottle about one quarter full of water, and put water likewise in the wash-bottle. Pour sulphuric acid down the long funnel, and gas will begin passing off almost immediately. This gas is hydrosulphuric acid. It is soluble in water, and must therefore be collected by displacement. It is heavier than air, so that the bottle must be arranged mouth upwards, as it was for chlorine. I do not advise you to make much of this gas. What you do make must be done out of doors, or in some place where the superfluous gas can pass readily away, for it is very poisonous, and has a most disgusting smell, like that of rotten eggs, the bad smell of which is in fact owing to this gas.

The following is the explanation of the process by which it is made :—

Sulphide of Iron.		Sulphuric Acid.		Protosulphate of Iron.		Hydrosulphuric Acid.
FeS	+	HO,SO_3	=	FeO,SO_3	+	HS.

After the mixture will give no more gas, a liquid is left in the generator, which, if it be evaporated down, will yield beautiful green crystals of protosulphate of iron (FeO,SO_3).

Hydrosulphuric acid is soluble in water, though not in very large quantity. You can prepare a solution by allowing the delivery-tube from which it is issuing to pass to the bottom of a bottle containing distilled water. When the water smells strongly of the gas, even after the bottle containing it has been shaken, and the loose gas on its surface blown away, it is sufficiently saturated.

Importance as a Test.—This gas is one of the most important *tests* with which chemists are acquainted. It forms insoluble compounds, called *sulphides*, with a good many of the metals, and consequently precipitates them from their solutions. Other metals, when they are in solution, are unaffected by it, and it therefore affords us a means of dividing the metallic oxides into two great classes.

If in any acid solution we obtain a black or coloured

precipitate on the addition of solution of hydrosulphuric acid, or on passing that gas through it, we may be sure that one or more of the following metals are present in it:—

Tin	Bismuth
Arsenic	Copper
Antimony	Mercury
Gold	Silver
Platinum	Some of the rarer
Lead	ones.

If hydrosulphuric acid produce no precipitate, of course none of the above metals can be present in the solution. In either case fresh tests may be applied.

Take three test-tubes, put into one a little solution of acetate of lead; into the second, a solution of sulphate of copper; and into the third, a solution of tartar emetic (tartrate of antimony and potash). Add a few drops of hydrochloric acid to each tube, and pour hydrosulphuric acid water into them until you can smell the gas strongly even after shaking. The lead and copper will both be precipitated as black sulphides, $Pb\,S$, and $Cu\,S$, while the antimony will give a bright orange precipitate of tersulphide, $Sb\,S_3$.

Hydrosulphuric acid is combustible. When a taper is applied to a bottle of it, it burns with a pale-blue flame. Sulphur is generally deposited on the sides of the bottle; but if enough oxygen be present, it is completely oxidized, water and sulphurous acid being produced:—

$$H\,S + 3\,O = H\,O + S\,O_2.$$

Test for Hydrosulphuric Acid.—The best test for the

presence of this gas is what is called "lead-paper." This is merely paper dipped in solution of acetate of lead, and dried. When it is moistened with water, and exposed to any gas or liquid which contains hydrosulphuric acid, it is instantly blackened from the formation of the sulphide of lead to which I have before adverted. A silver coin, or any other bright piece of silver, is likewise blackened from the same cause—the formation of a black sulphide of silver; and it is to the occasional presence of this gas in the air that the "tarnishing" of gold and silver articles, and the darkening of paints containing lead, is owing.

Hydrosulphuric acid is frequently given off from drains and stagnant pools, and is likewise a product of the putrefaction of animal matters, and is in a great measure the cause of the obnoxious smell of all three.

PHOSPHORUS, P = 32.

This curious and interesting element is never found native, but always in combination with some other element, and generally with oxygen. It is found in most minerals and plants; but by far its most important source is the bones of animals, of which it is an essential ingredient, in the form of phosphate of lime. From this it is obtained by treatment with sulphuric acid, and subsequent distillation of the dried mass with charcoal.

Properties.—When pure, it is a semi-transparent and wax-like substance, which can be cut with a knife, melts easily when heated under water, and inflames at a very slight elevation of temperature when heated in the air. In fact it is so combustible that it is always kept under water. When heated out of contact with air, it boils, and may be sublimed like sulphur.

In all experiments with phosphorus the greatest care is required, as it produces peculiarly painful burns.

Experiment 1.—You have already had occasion to observe the strong affinity which phosphorus has for oxygen. This is so intense as to cause it to combine with it even at ordinary temperatures, producing the luminous appearance which we have all observed when lucifer matches are rubbed in the dark. Take a small piece of phosphorus, hold it in a pair of tongs, or a porte-crayon, so that it cannot burn your hands if it should catch fire, and draw with it on a board in a dark room any words or figures you like. Do this very slowly and gently, and the phosphorus will not ignite. The writing will be found to be distinctly traced in letters of fire. This is owing to the slow oxidation of the phosphorus by the oxygen of the air. Though it is not perceptible by ordinary means, yet this oxidation is always attended by heat, which under suitable circumstances is enough to cause actual flame. The following experiment will illustrate this :—

Experiment 2.—Take a small stoppered bottle about half full of *bisulphide of carbon*. This liquid has the power of dissolving phosphorus. Put a few small pieces into the bottle, and they will soon disappear and produce a solution which has very singular properties. Pour a few drops on to a piece of paper. The liquid, being very volatile, will soon evaporate, and soon after it has done so, a sudden burst of flame will appear in the spots where the liquid touched. This flame will scorch the paper, but, strange to say, will not inflame it. The reason of the production of flame is, that when the bisulphide of carbon evaporates, it leaves the phosphorus in a finely divided state on the paper, and the oxygen of the air then attacks it so eagerly that flame results. The phosphorus is converted into phosphoric acid ($P\,O_5$), and this coats over the paper, and so prevents it from burning. If you spread a little powdered sulphur over the paper before you pour the solution of phosphorus on it, the phosphorus will combine with the sulphur, and the paper will be ignited. This is the reason that lucifer matches are always dipped in sulphur before the phosphorus tips are put on them.

Experiment 3.—To illustrate this last point more clearly, put a few small pieces of phosphorus on a piece of blotting-paper, and set fire to them. They will burn away and blacken the paper in doing so, but will not ignite it.

Experiment 4.—Put a few grains of chlorate of potash at the bottom of a tall glass. Fill the glass with water, and drop in a few grains of phosphorus. Take a pipette, that is a tube drawn out to a fine jet at one end, full of strong sulphuric acid, keeping the acid from running out by pressing your finger on the other end. Pass this pipette to the bottom of the glass, and then by removing your finger, allow a little acid to come in contact with the phosphorus and chlorate of potash. The phosphorus burns with beautiful flashes of light, even though it is below the surface of water, and this shows how energetic the action is.

Fig. 31.

Experiment 5.—Take a small and tightly stoppered bottle, and about one quarter fill it with sticks of phosphorus. Fill the bottle up with *ether*, and allow the whole to stand for a day or two, shaking it every now and then. The ether will dissolve a very little of the phosphorus, and acquire its property of luminosity in the dark.

1. Rub some of this solution on your hands and face, and look at yourself in a looking-glass in a dark room. You will find yourself converted into the most hideous object that you can well imagine; your eyes and mouth, which of course are not covered by the solution, looking like black spots on a sheet of blue flames. The experiment cannot possibly hurt you, provided you take care not to bring the phosphorized ether near a light. Ether is itself a very inflammable liquid, and that is the sole danger, for the quantity of phosphorus which dissolves in it, is so small, that it makes no difference in its inflammability.

2. Pour a few drops of the solution on a lump of sugar, and throw it into a tumbler of hot water in a dark room. No actual combustion, in the ordinary sense of the word, will take place, but the surface of the water will become most beautifully luminous, and bluish flames will play about on it like waves, especially if it be gently blown. I have already explained to you that all these beautiful effects are produced by slow combustion, or oxidation of the phosphorus.

Amorphous Phosphorus.
(*Red Phosphorus.*)

When phosphorus is heated for many hours at a temperature a little below its boiling-point, in a flask from which air has been removed by a current of carbonic acid, it is gradually converted into a peculiar *allotropic* form (v. page 44). In this state it is a dull-red, and rather heavy substance, which is quite insoluble in bisulphide of carbon and ether, and which does not exhibit the powerful affinity of common phosphorus for oxygen. For this reason it is not luminous in the dark, and may be carried about in the pocket, and even heated to more than twice the temperature of boiling water, without taking fire or combining with oxygen. When the heat is raised, however, to a little above this point, the red phosphorus is suddenly reconverted into common phosphorus, and then of course bursts into flame.

Amorphous phosphorus is acted on by chlorate of potash, just like common phosphorus (v. page 93, Ex. 3), and it has consequently been proposed as a substitute for the latter substance in lucifer matches. At present, however, it has not been found to answer very well.

Phosphoric Acid, PO_5.

Whenever phosphorus is burnt in a free supply either of air or of oxygen, this acid is produced. When pure, it is a white, snow-like powder, which, like sulphuric acid, manifests a most intense affinity for water. When it is exposed to the air, even for a few moments, it absorbs water so fast as to become liquid. This absorption of water from the air is called "deliquescence," and any solid substance which has this property is said to be "deliquescent." When dry phosphoric acid is thrown into water, it combines with it with explosive violence.

Hydrates of Phosphoric Acid.—The most curious fact about phosphoric acid is, that it combines with water in three definite proportions, producing compounds, each of which is a distinct acid, and has properties distinct from the others. It is not very easy for you to imagine how a substance which is soluble in water, and which will mix with it in any proportion, can yet form definite compounds with it, but so it is. I will give you an illustration, to show how this is possible. The crystals of common white alum, which we all know so well, and which dissolve so freely in water, do yet contain no less than twenty-four equivalents of water, even though they appear perfectly dry. These twenty-four equivalents of water are *combined* with the alum, just as I now tell you that water *combines* with phosphoric acid, though not precisely in the same way (v. page 73). The following are the compounds, or "hydrates," as they are called, of phosphoric acid and water:—

HO, PO_5, Monobasic phosphoric acid.
$2HO, PO_5$, Bibasic phosphoric acid.
$3HO, PO_5$, Tribasic, or common phosphoric acid.

Now in these three compounds, the water is considered to play the part of a weak base, and they are called monobasic, bibasic, and tribasic, because they contain one, two, and three equivalents of this base, water; and it is the more important to remember this fact, because all the salts which the three acids form with other bases, resemble them in this particular.

Thus, monobasic phosphoric acid requires only one equivalent of potash or soda, or any other base, to form a salt, and consequently we get such salts as these:—

HO, PO_5
KO, PO_5
NaO, PO_5

Bibasic phosphoric acid forms a set of salts with *two* equivalents of base:—

$2HOPO_5$
$2KOPO_5$
$2MgO, PO_5$

And, finally, tribasic phosphoric acid, which is by far the most common, never combines except with *three* equivalents. The phosphate of lime which is contained in bones is an instance of this; it is 3 CaO, PO_5—three equivalents of lime to one of phosphoric —not CaO, PO_5; and so it is with all others. Sometimes there are two, or even three different bases in the salt, as in the one which is called microcosmic salt, which may be represented thus:—

$$NaO, NH_4O, HO, PO_5.$$

Here, one of the three necessary equivalents of base, consists of soda, one of ammonia, and the remaining one of water. Again, with the common salt sold as phosphate of soda, and usually called so, even by chemists; it really contains:—

$$2\,NaO, HO, PO_5.$$

That is, two equivalents of soda, and one of water, to the one equivalent of phosphoric acid. Altogether, the phosphates form a very large, and very interesting class of salts. There are several other oxides of phosphorus, but none of any great importance.

Phosphoretted Hydrogen.

Put a little granulated zinc in a tall glass like that in fig. 31, fill it with water, and drop in two or three small pieces of phosphorus. Set the glass in a dark room, and pour in about a dram of sulphuric acid. In a few minutes, the most beautiful flashes of fire will shoot from the surface of the water in all directions, and luminous clouds will rise up from the glass. This pretty experiment has been very justly called the "fountain of fire." The explanation of it is, that the hydrogen, which was set free by the action of the zinc on the water (v. page 86), combines with a portion of the phosphorus, and forms the gas called "phosphoretted hydrogen," which has the property of spontaneous inflammability.*

SELENIUM.

Se = 39·5.

This is a very rare substance, closely resembling sulphur in its properties, but comparatively uninteresting. It was first discovered in some Swedish sulphur.

* It is doubtful whether this is the true explanation of this experiment. It has been asserted that the gas which burns, is only a mixture of hydrogen with the vapour of phosphorus.

CHAPTER IX.

CARBON, BORON, SILICON.

CARBON.

C = 6.

This element, like sulphur, is sometimes found in nature in a free state, and almost perfectly pure. It constitutes two minerals, which are so utterly unlike one another in their appearance and physical properties, that were it not for the evidence of chemical analysis, telling us that both were pure carbon, we should never dream of supposing that such was the case. These two minerals are, the diamond,—the beautiful and highly-valued precious stone, and the hardest substance in nature,—and graphite, or black-lead, as it is sometimes most incorrectly called, which is of such importance to us for the manufacture of lead pencils, and which is so soft that it can easily be cut with a knife, and even scratched with the finger-nail.

Besides these two substances, carbon in its compounds, is found in every department of nature. It forms a large and most essential part of all animal and vegetable bodies, and, in the shape of carbonic acid, is an important ingredient of those chalk rocks, with which the shores of our country are lined in so many places.

You already know that it is present in air; water is seldom free from it, and all the various kinds of coal, coke, and charcoal are mainly composed of it. These facts will enable you to judge of its vast importance in the economy of nature.

Properties.—Carbon, from whatever source obtained, has the same *chemical* properties. It is utterly infusible, even at the highest temperature, and cannot be made to volatilize or sublime. Its most important property by far, however, is that of combining readily with oxygen under the influence of heat; it is this which gives it its value as fuel. Charcoal, which, as you know, is one form of carbon, has likewise the very valuable property of absorbing gases into its pores, and this is found to render it useful as a *disinfectant* and *deodorizing* agent. All bad and noxious smells are caused by small quantities of gases or vapours in the air. These appear to be absorbed and destroyed by the charcoal, and the same effect is produced in many liquids, and even solids. If a piece of bad meat be covered over with recently prepared charcoal powder, and allowed to stand for some time, the bad smell will entirely disappear, and the meat be made quite sweet and fit for use.

Oxides of Carbon.

The most important of these are—

Carbonic Oxide	CO
Oxalic Acid	C_2O_3
Carbonic Acid	CO_2

Carbonic Oxide, CO.—This compound, which is a

gas, may be procured from the second oxide, oxalic acid, by the following process:—Oxalic acid itself is a substance of vegetable origin, found in salts of sorrel (binoxalate of potash), and generally prepared from sugar or starch.

Take the apparatus represented in fig. 32, connect the delivery-tube, *b*, with the wash-bottle of the hydrogen apparatus, and replace the water of the latter, by a solution of potash. Put into the flask an ounce or two of crystals of oxalic acid, pour five or six ounces of strong sulphuric acid on it, through the funnel, and apply a gentle heat to the sand-bath.

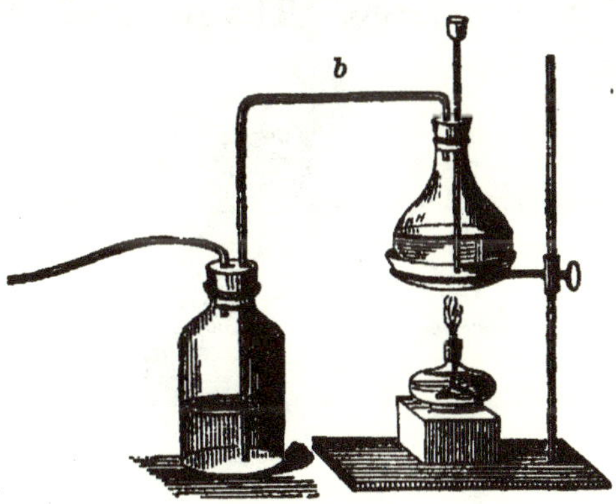

Fig. 32.

The gas may be collected over water. Now, the explanation of the process is this:—

$$HO, C_2 O_3 + HO, SO_3 = CO + CO_2 + 2\, HO, SO_3.$$

Oxalic acid, I have just told you, consists of $C_2 O_3$, and it is always combined with water, so that its symbol is $HO, C_2 O_3$. Now $C_2 O_3$ is evidently the same as $CO + CO_2$, so that when the sulphuric acid takes the water from the crystals, CO and CO_2, or carbonic oxide and carbonic acid, rise as gases. The carbonic acid is absorbed by the potash in the wash-bottle, forming with it carbonate of potash, while the carbonic oxide passes through it unchanged.

Properties.—Carbonic oxide is a colourless, almost odourless, and very poisonous gas. It is a little lighter than air, is not a supporter of combustion, but is a combustible body.

Take a bottle of the gas, and apply a light to its mouth. It will burn with a beautiful blue flame, and if water be poured quickly into the bottle, the flame will be very large. The result of the combus-

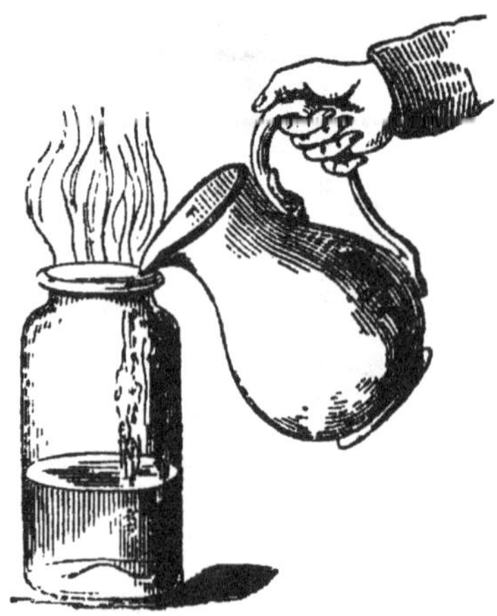

Fig. 33.

tion is carbonic acid, the carbonic oxide taking one equivalent of oxygen from the air:—

$$CO + O = CO_2.$$

Carbonic Acid, CO_2.—You have already heard a good deal about this important body. You know that it is the usual product of the combustion of carbon, and of substances which contain it; and you know, likewise, that it is present in considerable quantities in the air, being exhaled from the lungs of animals. I will now show you how to prepare it. This can be done in a manner exactly similar to hydrogen, and the same apparatus will do, but instead of zinc and water, you must use lumps of marble or chalk (carbonate of lime) and water; and instead of sulphuric acid, hydrochloric acid. The gas is very heavy, half as heavy again as common air, and as it is soluble in water, it must be collected like chlorine, by displacement.

The following is the explanation of the process by which it is obtained:—

$$\underset{\text{Carbonate of Lime.}}{CaO, CO_2} + \underset{\text{Hydrochloric Acid.}}{HCl} = \underset{\text{Chloride of Calcium.}}{CaCl} + \underset{\text{Water.}}{HO} + \underset{\text{Carbonic Acid.}}{CO_2}.$$

A solution of chloride of calcium remains in the generator.

Experiment 1.—Carbonic acid is incombustible, and a non-supporter of combustion. Plunge a lighted taper into a bottle of it, and it will immediately be extinguished.

Experiment 2.—Carbonic acid is very heavy. This can be shown by filling a jar open at the top, by displacement, and then bucketing the gas out with a beaker tied to a glass rod. A lighted taper dipped in the "bucket," after it is taken out full of gas, is found to be extinguished, showing that the gas remains in the glass just as though it were a liquid.

Experiment 3.—The weight of carbonic acid can be shown very prettily by pouring the gas out from a small jar, or the bucket used in the preceding experiment, on to a lighted taper standing on the table. Though the gas is quite invisible, this can easily be done, and the effect is very striking. The taper at once goes out.

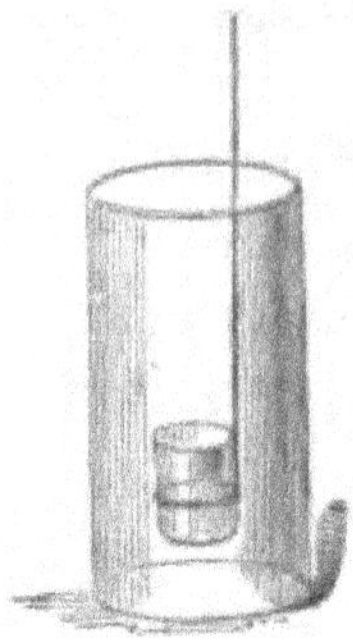

Fig. 34.

It is to the escape of carbonic acid that soda-water and other effervescing drinks owe their agreeable pungency, and its solution is quite harmless when drank, although the gas is so poisonous when taken into the lungs.

Coal Gas.

Carbon forms a great many very important compounds with hydrogen, but it is impossible at present even to allude to more than one or two.

The common mineral which we call coal, and which has been produced in the course of ages from decayed vegetable bodies, such as trees and large ferns, is composed of only a very few elements, and principally of three,—carbon, oxygen, and hydrogen.

Its other constituents are, small quantites of sulphur, nitrogen, and mineral ash. Now, when coal is distilled in retorts without the access of air, it is decomposed, and a number of volatile products pass off. A portion of these products, namely, the tar and water, are condensed into the liquid form when the gas cools, but the remainder are permanent gases, and can be collected and used as fuel. This "destructive distillation," as it is called, of the coal, can be shown on a small scale by the old experiment of the tobacco-pipe. Most people know it, but I shall describe it for the benefit of any who may not.

Take a common long tobacco-pipe, put a little cinder into the bottom of the bowl, and nearly fill it with powdered coal. Cover the mouth of the bowl over with soft clay, and let it dry gently before a fire. Then stick the bowl of the pipe into the fire, with the end projecting into the room. In a minute or two, gas, accompanied with smoke, will issue from the long end of the pipe, and may be lighted by a match. It will burn brightly for several minutes: when the flame has gone out, take the pipe out of the fire, and knock out what is left in the bowl. The coal will be found to be converted into a mass of coke. If this coke were to be analysed, it would be found to consist almost entirely of carbon, the whole of the oxygen and hydrogen, together with a portion of the carbon, having passed off in a volatile form.

Now let us consider the nature of these volatile bodies. The liquid portion consists, as I told you before, of tar and water. The gases are numerous, but the most important by far are two "hydrocarbons," or compounds of carbon and hydrogen. They are called,—

Heavy carburetted hydrogen, or olefiant gas . . . . C_4H_4,
Light carburetted hydrogen, or marsh gas . . . . C_2H_4,

and the second is always present in much the greater quantity.

Besides these, a number of gases, small in amount, but either useless or injurious in their nature, are always present. The most important of the injurious ones are carbonic acid, hydrosulphuric acid, and ammonia. When gas is made on a large scale for use as a source of light and heat, it is of course highly important that these injurious gases should be separated from it. This is effected in the following manner:—The coal is distilled in large retorts, generally made of iron. The products are carried first into an iron cylinder, which is called the hydraulic main. In this a great deal of the tar and water is condensed, and as ammonia is soluble in water, a good deal of that too remains in solution in the water, and it is principally this which causes the disagreeable smell of "gas-water." Both the tar and gas-water are now subjected to processes by which valuable substances are obtained from them. The beautiful colour called "mauve," which has been so fashionable of late, is usually obtained from the black, dirty, and foul-smelling coal-tar.

When the gas leaves the hydraulic main, it is conducted through a series of long and bent iron pipes, in which it is cooled, and a further portion of tar, water, and ammonia deposited. It is then passed through a chamber filled with lime, either dry or mixed with water. The lime absorbs the carbonic acid, hydrosulphuric acid, and some other impurities, and leaves the gas fit for use.

The large, black, iron cylinders which we see in the yards of gas-works, are called "gas-holders." Their use is merely to store the gas when it is made, and to insure a uniform pressure on the pipes by which the gas is conveyed through the town.

The two gases which I have mentioned as forming the chief part of coal gas, can both be obtained perfectly pure. They are then entirely scentless, the strong smell of common gas being owing to certain volatile impurities which it contains. These impurities, however, act a very important part in the gas, for without their strong and unpleasant smell, we should never know when gas was escaping into a room, and consequently should run no slight risk of being blown up. Both light and heavy carburetted hydrogen are converted by burning into carbonic acid and water: the former gas, as its name implies, is much lighter than air; the latter is only a very little lighter.

Nature of Flame.

1. If you take a candle, snuff it rather short, so as to get a clear, steady flame, and observe this attentively, you will see that in the centre, just above the wick, there is a black portion. Above this the bright part comes, and outside of all a pale zone or envelope of yellow flame. These three

zones are to be seen not only in the flame of a candle; they may be observed with coal gas, with oil, and spirit-lamps, and, in fact, in all cases where carbon is contained in the fuel. They are called respectively:—

The zone of *no* combustion,—Inner portion.

The zone of *partial* combustion,—Middle portion.

The zone of *complete* combustion,—Outer portion.

The inner one is called the zone of *no* combustion, because in it the gases given out by the fuel are not burnt at all, there being there no oxygen wherewith to oxidize them. This you can prove very easily by holding a slip of wood for a few seconds across the flame of a candle, and just above the wick. The wood will be charred only at the outer edges of the flame, the inner portion remaining white. A piece of white paper pressed down on the wick of the candle for an instant, will have a black ring marked on it. The middle zone is the region where partial

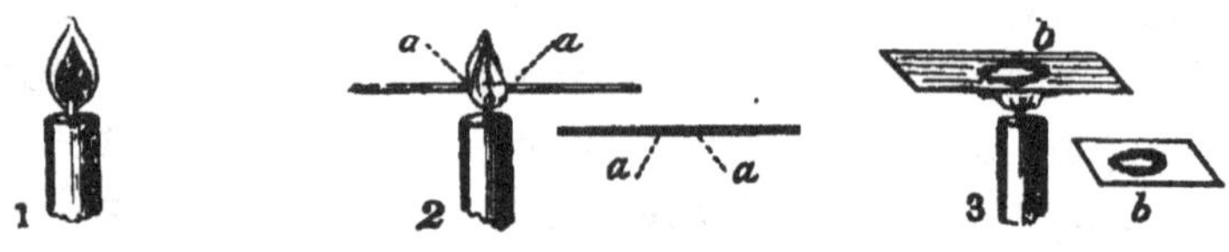

Fig. 35.—1 is the candle flame with its three zones; 2 is the candle with the stick held in it; *a* shows the points at which it is blackened; 3 is the paper with the blackened ring *b* on it.

combustion goes on, by the partial access of air. In the outer zone the gases are completely oxidized by the free supply of oxygen yielded by the air.

2. The *light* given by a flame depends almost entirely on the presence of minute particles of carbon, or some other solid matter suspended in it. The flame of hydrogen, you remember, gives scarcely any

light, and that of a spirit-lamp is not much better in this respect. Now if you sprinkle a little charcoal powder, or iron-filings in either of these flames, they will become, for the instant, quite bright. This is because the solid particles are heated white hot, and in that state throw out a good deal of light.

Coal-gas consists entirely of carbon and hydrogen. When the gas burns, the hydrogen combines with the oxygen of the air more rapidly than the carbon does, and the latter remains therefore for an instant in minute particles suspended at a white heat in the middle zone of the flame. The particles then pass into the outer zone, and are at once oxidized by the air, but fresh particles constantly succeed them, and in this way the flame is maintained.

3. If you take the flame of a spirit-lamp, and direct a jet of air from your lungs through it by means of a *blow-pipe*, a little instrument which can be procured almost anywhere, the flame will be bent in a curious way, and entirely altered in its structure.

Fig. 36.

The blow-pipe is to be held in the right hand, and its jet at the edge of the flame, just above the wick. A continuous stream of air should be forced through it by puffing the cheeks out, and refilling them from time to time with air from the lungs. This can only be learnt by practice; the great thing in beginning is not to blow too hard. If this blow-pipe flame be examined, it will be found to consist of only two parts, a blue inner cone and a yellow outer one. There is no "zone of no combustion" in this case, because oxygen is projected into the very centre of the flame. The inner cone consists of carbonic oxide, which you remember (v. page 118) burns with a blue flame. It is being converted into carbonic acid by absorbing oxygen from the air, or from whatever is presented to it. This inner flame is generally called the "reducing flame," from the curious fact of its having the property of reducing some metallic oxides to the metallic state. This it does by causing them to contribute their oxygen towards the oxidation of the carbonic oxide, of which, as I told you, the flame is composed. The outer or yellow flame is known as the "oxidizing flame," from its possessing exactly the opposite properties from the inner one, namely, the property of causing the oxidation, at the expense of the air, of many metals heated in it.

To illustrate the properties of these two flames, take a little red oxide of lead (red lead), put it in a small hole in the side of a piece of charcoal, and expose it to the inner, or reducing, blow-pipe flame. In a few moments the red substance will disappear, and instead of it you will obtain a small bright bead of metallic lead. If this be now exposed to the outer, or oxidizing flame, it will be reconverted into oxide of lead. The blow-pipe is an instrument of very great use to chemists. If, instead of common air, a current of oxygen be forced through the flame, and especially if hydrogen be used instead of a common flame, a most intense heat is produced. This is called the oxy-hydrogen blow-pipe, and the most infusible substances, such as platinum and quartz, are very speedily fused by it. When it is directed on a piece of quick-lime, though the lime is neither fused nor burned, it is raised to such an intensely white heat as to produce the beautiful light called the lime light, which has been recently used for illuminating the new Westminster Bridge.

Davy Lamp.—Light carburetted hydrogen is very often given out from between the layers of coal in coal-mines. This collects in the galleries and passages of the mines, and constitutes the "fire-damp," which is such a deadly enemy to the poor miner. It mixes with the common air, and when a light is introduced into the mixture, a terrific explosion follows. This is not the only danger; for the combustion of the fire-damp produces, as you have before learned, carbonic acid, and this poisonous gas, which is called "choke-damp" by the miners, very frequently suffocates those who escape from the explosion.

Of course it had always been a most important object to discover some means of lighting the miners at their work, without the risk of these fearful explosions; but till Sir Humphry Davy discovered the principles upon which the lamp which is named after him is constructed, no one succeeded. He proved that a white heat is necessary to maintain the flame of fire-damp, and that if the temperature of the flame be reduced below this point, it goes out. This is the reason that a candle or lamp can be blown out by a sudden blast of air. The cold air cools the flame below the point at which combustion can go on, and so it is extinguished. It is for this reason that flame will not pass through a wire gauze. The gases will pass through it readily enough, but the wire gauze absorbs heat so fast from the flame, that combustion cannot go on. You can prove this important fact by pressing a piece of iron-wire gauze down on a gas or spirit flame (the former is the best). The effect is shown at *a*, fig. 37. If you blow out the flame, and hold the gauze a little above the jet or wick, you can relight it by applying a light on the other side, as seen at *b*. The flame will not pass downwards any more than it will upwards.

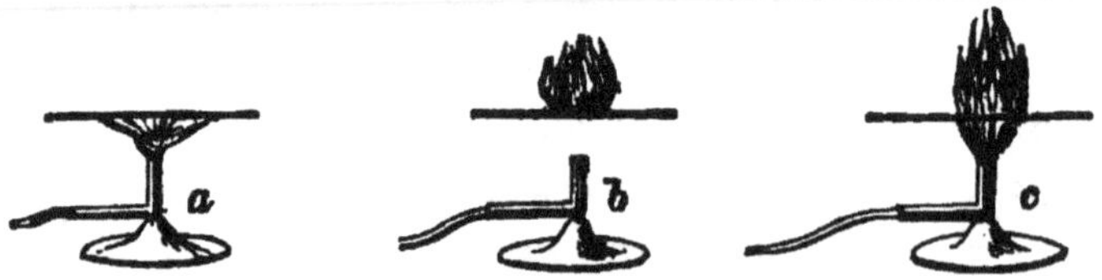

Fig. 37.

In either case, if a light be applied to the other side as well, the flame will burn as usual, as at *c*.

The Davy-lamp consists of a common oil-lamp, entirely surrounded by wire gauze. The air passes in freely through this, and allows the lamp to burn. When the air of the mine becomes so much mixed with fire-damp (carburetted hydrogen) as to be inflammable, it passes in with the air to the lamp, and there catches fire. With any common lamp the flame so produced would immediately spread to the gas outside, and produce a general conflagration; but the wire gauze stops the flame from passing for the reason I have already told you, and renders an accident very unlikely to occur. As soon as the miner finds the

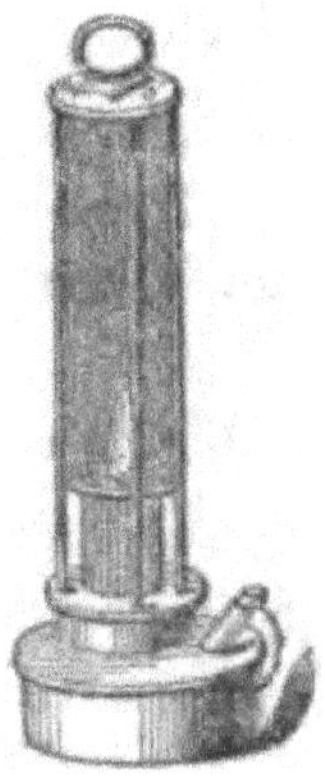

Fig. 38.

gas is burning inside his lamp, he should make haste and leave the place, as it would not be safe to remain there afterwards, the wire gauze being liablo occasionally to break into holes.

Bisulphide of Carbon, CS_2.

I have already more than once adverted to this curious liquid. It is formed by distilling together sulphur and charcoal. It is a transparent and colourless liquid, which is very volatile and exceedingly inflammable. It burns with a blue flame, very difficult to extinguish, and is converted into carbonic and sulphurous acids. It is likewise remarkable for its disgusting odour.

The following experiment is an interesting one.—

Get some very thin steel wire—that sold as "harpsichord wire" is the best—and break it into pieces about eight inches long; make these pieces into a little brush, and hold one end of this brush in the flame of some bisulphide of carbon burning in a cup or small basin. The iron will soon inflame, and will burn with most beautiful sparks. In this experiment, the sulphur of the bisulphide of carbon, combines with the iron, forming *sulphide of iron.*

BORON, Bo = 10·9.

This is an element which appears to resemble carbon very closely in its physical properties, having been recently obtained in two crystalline shapes, one of which is as hard as the diamond, and very like it, while the other is similar to graphite. Boron derives its chief importance from its being the basis of *Boracic Acid*, $Bo\ O_3$, a rather important acid, found in Tuscany.

Borax, $Na\ O, 2\ Bo\ O_3$, is a compound of boracic acid with two equivalents of soda.

SILICON, Si = 21·3.

This element, which, like the preceding, is only to be procured by a difficult process, may be obtained in three distinct shapes. Its main interest is derived from its oxide.

Silicic Acid, $Si\ O_3$.—This is one of the most important minerals found in nature, and likewise one of the most abundant. Colourless rock-crystal or quartz, is nearly pure silicic acid, and flint, agate, calcedony, and many other minerals, are mainly composed of it. Glass is a mixture of several *silicates*, or compounds of silicic acid with bases; and silicic acid is likewise found, in greater or less quantities, in nearly all animals, vegetables, and minerals.

There are no very striking experiments to be done with silicic acid.

CHAPTER X.

THE METALS.

General Physical Characteristics.

One of the most important characters of a metal is the "metallic lustre." This is the peculiar brightness which all metals possess, and which is familiar to all of us, though it is almost impossible to describe. It is distinct from mere colour, for copper and silver, which differ entirely in colour, both alike possess it. It is not to be considered as solely confined to metals, for more than one of the non-metallic elements possess it in a greater or less degree, but still, speaking generally, we say that it is an attribute of metals.

As to *weight*, metals vary very much indeed. Platinum, which is the heaviest substance known, is about twenty-one times heavier than water; gold, about nineteen times; silver, ten times; copper, nearly nine times; iron, eight times; while sodium, potassium, and lithium, are actually lighter than that liquid. The last of these is the lightest solid known.

Metals, generally speaking, are quite opaque. When beaten into very thin leaves, gold allows a little light to pass through it, and then appears of a splendid purple colour. Professor Faraday has recently exhibited this in a very beautiful manner.

Metals likewise differ very much in the property of *malleability* (from malleus, a hammer), or power of extension, when hammered or rolled out. Many metals, such as bismuth, antimony, and arsenic are quite brittle, and may be powdered with a mortar and pestle, while others, such as gold, silver, and tin, can be beaten out into amazingly thin plates. Gold is by far the most perfect metal in this respect; it will bear much more hammering than any other metal, and in consequence of its great value this property is made use of to the greatest possible extent. One grain of gold can be hammered into fifty-two square inches of gold-leaf, or drawn into five hundred and fifty feet of wire. This last fact is rather an instance of the *ductility* of gold than its malleability.

The *fusibility* of metals is also very different. Potassium and sodium melt at temperatures below that of boiling water; tin and lead, below a red heat; copper and silver, at a bright red heat; and gold and iron, only at a white heat; while others, such as platinum, rhodium, and titanium, cannot be melted even in the most powerful furnaces, but require the intenser heat of the oxy-hydrogen blow-pipe.

Metallic Combinations.

1. *With each other.*—Most, if not all, of the metals are capable of combining with one another. The compounds they form are called *alloys*, and some of them are of very great importance. For instance, brass is an alloy of copper and zinc; gun-metal and bell-metal are alloys in different proportions

of copper and tin; and common pewter is an alloy of tin and lead. Some of the alloys which iron forms with the rarer metals, such as rhodium, are very interesting, and if they were not so expensive would be most useful in the arts. It has been recently proposed to employ an alloy of iron with a small proportion of the metal tungsten, for making the new Armstrong guns. It appears to increase the strength of the guns most remarkably.

When mercury combines with another metal, the compound is not called an alloy, but an *amalgam*. Thus we speak of the amalgam of gold, the amalgam of silver, and the amalgam of tin, meaning thereby the compounds of those metals with mercury. The last of these amalgams, the amalgam of tin, is the one which is used in silvering looking-glasses.

2. *With the non-metallic elements.*—The metals form a large and very important class of compounds with the non-metallic elements.

The following are the most important series:—

Oxygen . .	produces .	Oxides.
Chlorine .	„ .	Chlorides.
Iodine . .	„ .	Iodides.
Bromine .	„ .	Bromides.
Fluorine .	„ .	Fluorides.
Sulphur .	„ .	Sulphides.
Phosphorus	„ .	Phosphides.
Carbon . .	„ .	Carbides.

Of these, the *oxides* form by far the most important set of compounds. I have already (page 43) told you something about them; that they are divided into acid, neutral, and basic oxides. The first and last of these classes give rise to an immense number of compounds, some of them of the highest importance, which are called salts. I shall have more to say about these very soon.

The *chlorides*, *iodides*, *bromides*, and *fluorides* resemble each other very closely in their general characters. The chlorides are the most important.

These four classes of compounds are generally grouped together as *haloid salts* (v. page 96), while the sulphides, phosphides, and other classes are not considered as coming under that term. The propriety of this arrangement is, however, somewhat doubtful. The *sulphides* and *phosphides* exhibit a certain amount of similarity to one another.

Constitution of Oxy-salts (v. page 85).

Salts, that is compounds of acids and bases, are of three different kinds. These three kinds are distinguished as neutral, acid, and basic salts.

Meaning of Neutrality.—If you moisten blue litmus paper with *nitric acid*, the paper, as you already know, is turned red. On the other hand, if red litmus paper be moistened with solution of *potash*, it is turned blue. Now, take a solution of *nitrate of potash*, which is a compound of these two, and dip in it first blue, and then red litmus paper. Neither of them will be affected by the solution, showing that the *acid* properties of nitric acid, and the *basic* properties of potash, have both been destroyed, or *neutralised* by their union together; nitrate of potash is a *neutral* salt.

But supposing instead of the powerful base potash, the nitric acid had been combined with the weak base *oxide of lead*; on dipping blue litmus paper into a solution of this compound, *nitrate of lead*, we should have found it reddened, because the strong acid had, as it were, overmastered the weak base.

On the contrary, suppose the potash, the powerful base, had been combined with a weak acid, such as *carbonic acid*, the resulting compound, *carbonate of potash*, would have turned red litmus to blue, the base overpowering the acid. But now let us look at the formulæ for the three salts we have been considering.

Nitrate of potash . . .	KO, NO_5
Nitrate of lead	PbO, NO_5
Carbonate of potash . .	KO, CO_2

You see that the proportions of acid and base are the same in all three cases. They are all arranged in *equivalent* proportion, and therefore they are regarded by chemists as *neutral salts*, even when their physical properties are powerfully acid, or powerfully basic.

Polybasic Acids.—In speaking of phosphoric acid (page 112), I have told you of two of its hydrates which possess the properties of distinct acids, and which require more than one equivalent of base to neutralize them. These acids, the bibasic and tribasic phosphoric acids, are representatives of an important class, which are called *polybasic acids* (from *polos*, many). Of this class are many of the vegetable acids. Tartaric acid, for example, is bibasic, and citric acid (the acid contained in lemons) is tribasic.

With all these polybasic acids, a neutral salt can only be obtained by causing the right number of equivalents of base to combine with the acid. Thus the following are neutral salts:—$\overline{T}$ stands for tartaric acid, and $\overline{Ci}$ for citric acid. The vegetable acids are often so represented:—

$2\,KO, PO_5$ = Phosphate of potash. (Bibasic variety.)
$3\,KO, PO_5$ = Phosphate of potash. (Tribasic variety.)
$2\,KO, \overline{T}$ = Tartrate of potash.
$3\,KO, \overline{Ci}$ = Citrate of potash.

Law of Neutrality.—Well then, leaving these polybasic acids, which are to be regarded as exceptional cases, out of the question, the following is the rule for the proportion of acid and base necessary to form a neutral salt:—

In a neutral salt there are always as many equivalents of acid as there are equivalents of oxygen in the base.

Thus in the following salts,—

KO, NO_5 . . . Nitrate of potash,
PbO, NO_5 . . . Nitrate of lead,
FeO, SO_3 . . . Sulphate of iron,
KO, CrO_3 . . . Chromate of potash,

there is one equivalent of oxygen in each of the bases, and consequently each salt contains one equivalent of acid.

There are some bases which contain more oxygen

than the above, and these by the same rule require more acid.

$Fe_2O_3, 3SO_3$ . .	Sesquisulphate of iron, or, more correctly, sulphate of the sesquioxide of iron.
$Al_2O_3, 3SO_3$ . .	Sulphate of alumina. (Sulphate of the sesquioxide of aluminum.)
$BiO_3, 3NO_5$ . .	Ternitrate of bismuth. (Nitrate of the teroxide of bismuth.)

These salts, remember, are all neutral.

Acid Salts.—When a salt contains more of any acid (not a polybasic one) than the preceding rule requires, it is called an *acid salt.*

$KO, 2CrO_3$ . . .	Bichromate of potash.
$NaO, 2BoO_3$. . .	Biborate of soda.

Basic Salts.—When a salt contains more base than the law requires, it is called a *basic salt.*

$2PbO, NO_5$ . . .	Dinitrate of lead.
$3HgO, NO_5$ . . .	Trisnitrate of mercury.

Classification of Metals.

I shall divide the metals into three great classes. A more scientific arrangement is generally adopted, but I think the present will be more convenient for beginners. I have only included the most important of them.

Class I.

Metals of the Alkalies and Earths.

Potassium.	Calcium.
Sodium.	Magnesium.
Barium.	Aluminum.
Strontium.	

Class II.

Metals Proper, Fusible below a Red Heat.

Lead.	Bismuth.
Tin.	Zinc.
Arsenic.	Mercury.
Antimony.	

Class III.

Metals Proper, Infusible below a Red Heat.

Iron.	Copper.
Manganese.	Tungsten.
Chromium.	Silver.
Cobalt.	Platinum.
Nickel.	Gold.

Class I.

Metals of the Alkalies and Earths.

Potassium, K = 39.

You have already heard and seen so much of this beautiful and interesting metal, that many of its properties are familiar to you. It is a blue and very light metal, forming the basis of potash, and having so intense an affinity for oxygen, that it is capable of separating it from almost every one of its combinations.

Till the time of Sir Humphry Davy, every attempt to decompose the "fixed alkalies," as potash and soda are called, had failed. In was in the year 1800 that the Royal Institution of Great Britain was first established, and it was in the following year that Humphry Davy, then only twenty-two years old, was appointed lecturer on chemistry, and director of the chemical laboratory to that since celebrated institution. He worked with the most indomitable perseverance, and the most brilliant success. Some experiments on voltaic electricity which he made in the years 1806 and 1807, suggested to his mind the idea of employing this powerful agent in endeavouring to decompose the alkalies. In October of the latter year, this idea was reduced to practice by exposing a small piece of potash to the action of the powerful voltaic battery which belonged to the institution. To the intense joy of Davy, the potash began to melt, violent effervescence took place on its upper surface, from the escape of oxygen, and on the lower surface "small bright globules resembling quicksilver appeared, some of which were no sooner formed than they burnt with explosion and bright flame. He had decomposed potash, and obtained its base in a metallic form."

Potassium is now prepared in large quantities by distilling together in an iron retort carbonate of potash and charcoal. The carbon takes the oxygen from the potash, and the metal distils over, and is received in a vessel containing naphtha and surrounded by ice. It is subsequently purified by redistillation. It is always kept under naphtha, as when exposed to the air, it almost instantly becomes covered with a coating of oxide.

Oxide of Potassium—Potash, KO.—The most powerful base known. This substance is produced when potassium is exposed to perfectly dry air or oxygen. It has a strong affinity for water, and forms with it a definite hydrate, KO, HO; the water, as is always the case when it is in combination with a base, performing the part of a weak acid. This water cannot afterwards be expelled from it by any degree of heat. Hydrate of potash is generally prepared by adding hydrate of lime to a solution of carbonate of potash:—

$$KO, CO_2 + CaO, HO = KO, HO + CaO, CO_2.$$

Carbonate of lime falls as an insoluble precipitate, and may be separated by filtration. The liquid is evaporated in a silver or iron vessel to dryness, and fused. It is then suffered to cool, when it solidifies to a white hard mass. This is the hydrate of potash. Hydrate of potash is a most powerfully caustic and alkaline substance. It attacks and destroys most animal and vegetable substances.

Take a little piece of raw meat, a piece of bladder, a linen rag, and a slip of paper; soak them all for a short time in solution of potash. You will find that they have all become quite rotten in the process.

All non-volatile oils and fats, such as olive oil,

train oil, tallow, and lard, are converted into *soaps* of different kinds, and become soluble in water, when boiled with potash.

All the potash soaps are of the kind called "soft soap;" the ordinary hard soaps are made with soda instead of potash.

Solution of potash precipitates from their solutions, all metallic oxides which are not soluble in water, and it is therefore a most important test in analytical chemistry. I will illustrate this by a few experiments.

Take a little solution of each of the following salts:—sesquichloride of iron ($Fe_2 Cl_3$), acetate of lead, sulphate of nickel, chloride of mercury (corrosive sublimate, Hg Cl), and sulphate of copper. Put these solutions into test-tubes, and add to each a few drops of the solution of potash. You will get precipitates of the following colours:—

Lead	White . . .	Pb O, H O.
Iron (sesquioxide)	Red	$Fe_2 O_3$, 3 H O.
Nickel	Green . . .	Ni O, H O.
Mercury (peroxide)	Yellow . . .	Hg O, H O.
Copper	Blue . . .	Cu O, H O.

These precipitates consist of the *hydrates* of the oxides of the metals. You will see by the above table that hydrates observe the law of neutrality which I explained at page 137. They are in fact salts, with water for their acid.

If you pour a little more potash on the lead precipitate, and shake the tube for a little while, it will dissolve up again. This is called being "soluble in excess," and is a very common occurrence.

Potash and all other compounds of potassium, impart a violet colour to the blow-pipe flame. This test of the colour of a flame is sometimes a very important one. It is thus conducted:—

Take a piece of thin platinum wire a few inches long. Make a small hook at one end of it, moisten this hook with a drop of a solution of some salt of potash, and hold it in the blow-pipe flame just at the point of the inner or reducing flame. A faint violet tint will be observed in the usually yellow, outer flame. If the colour be not seen at once, dip the wire again and again into the solution, until enough of it has been taken up.

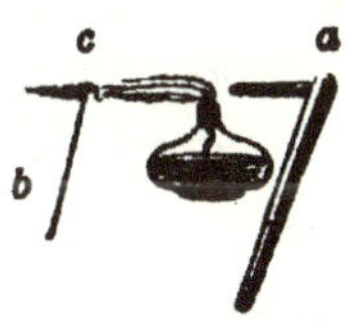

Fig. 39.—*a* is the blow-pipe; *b* the platinum wire; *c* the portion of flame coloured.

Coloured Flames.—While I am on the subject of coloured flames, I may as well tell you of one or two others. If the wire be dipped into a solution containing strontium (nitrate of strontia, for instance), a beautiful *red* flame will be produced. Copper (sulphate, or better still, chloride) gives a bright *green* flame, while sodium (common salt) gives a *yellow* one. The same substances, when dissolved in spirits of wine, impart their colours to the flame of that liquid. The experiment is so pretty that I shall describe it.

Dissolve a little common salt, nitrate of strontia, and chloride of copper in three different portions of spirits of wine, or common wood-naphtha. Put these solutions into small basins, light the spirit, and stir it while it burns. They will burn with the same colours as were imparted to the blow-pipe flame. If you make little mops by fastening cotton wool to the end of wires, and dip these mops in the solutions, and then light them, the effect will be still more beautiful.

The splendid red fire which is used at theatres and in fireworks depends for its colour on strontium. The following is a good receipt for making it:—

Nitrate of strontia . . .	10	ounces.
Chlorate of potash . .	$1\frac{1}{2}$	,,
Flowers of sulphur . .	$3\frac{1}{2}$	,,
Sulphide of antimony .	1	,,
Charcoal powder . . .	$\frac{1}{2}$	,,

Dry the nitrate of strontia first in a basin on a sand-bath thoroughly. This will very likely take some time. Then reduce it to fine powder. The chlorate of potash is likewise to be powdered separately, as are also the other constituents, which must all be perfectly dry. The whole are then mixed together with a card, as they are apt to explode with friction.

For green fire this is the receipt:—

Nitrate of baryta . . .	10	ounces.
Chlorate of potash . .	$\frac{3}{4}$	,,
Flowers of sulphur . .	$1\frac{1}{8}$	,,
Sulphide of antimony .	$\frac{1}{2}$	,,
Charcoal powder . . .	$\frac{1}{4}$	,,

The mixture is made exactly in the same way as for red fire.

Salts of Potash.—These are very numerous, and many of them very important. You have already heard much of the nitrate and the chlorate (v. pages 79 and 92). The former of these, which is also known as nitre and saltpetre, is of the highest value for the manufacture of gunpowder, of which it is the principal constituent. English gunpowder is usually composed of—

Nitre	75 parts.
Charcoal	15 ,,
Sulphur	10 ,,

When it is burnt it is converted into carbonic acid, free nitrogen, and sulphide of potassium, which last is the cause of the disagreeable smell left in a cannon or gun-barrel after a discharge.

The carbonate, sulphate, and bichromate of potash are likewise important salts.

Other Compounds of Potassium.—Potassium forms haloid salts with chloride, iodine, and bromine. The iodide of potassium is now of great importance from its use in photography.

Sodium, Na = 23.

This metal strongly resembles potassium in most respects. It is obtained from carbonate of soda in the same manner as potassium. The process, however, is easier. It is a white and very soft metal, lighter than water, which it floats upon and decomposes (v. page 62).

Oxide of Sodium, Soda, NaO.—This is obtained from

the carbonate in exactly the same manner as potash, which it closely resembles in appearance and properties. Its hydrate, NaO, HO, is, like the hydrate of potash, very deliquescent.

Salts of Soda.—Many of these are of the very highest importance, not only in our every-day life, but also for manufacturing purposes. They are all more or less soluble in water.

Carbonate of Soda, NaO, CO_2.—This, which was formerly obtained almost exclusively from the ashes of sea-weed, is now prepared in enormous quantities from common salt. Unlike carbonate of potash, which is deliquescent, carbonate of soda is *efflorescent;* that is, the crystals, instead of absorbing water from the air, and so becoming liquid, give what water they possess, out to the air, and gradually crumble into a dry white powder.

If two basins be exposed to the air, one of which contains carbonate of potash, and the other crystals of carbonate of soda, their difference in this respect will be clearly seen in a short time.

Sulphate of Soda, NaO, SO_3, is largely used in medicine by the name of Glauber's salt.

Nitrate of Soda, NaO, NO_5, is found native in enormous beds in Chili. It is valuable for the manufacture of nitric acid, but will not answer for gunpowder, as the mixture burns too slowly, and is apt to get damp.

Phosphates of Soda.—There are several of these. The one which is generally known and sold by this name is the tribasic phosphate, containing one equivalent of water, $2NaO, HO, PO_5$.

Other Compounds of Sodium.—The most important by far is the *chloride*, Na Cl, or common salt, which, besides the vast supply existing in sea water, is found in some parts of the world in immense beds. It crystallizes in cubes. All sodium compounds impart a yellow colour to flame.

BARIUM, Ba = 68·5.

This metal can be obtained by a difficult process, which consists in passing the vapour of potassium over baryta, heated to bright redness in an iron tube. The reduced metal is extracted with mercury, which is subsequently separated from it by distillation. It is a good deal like sodium, though it does not melt at so low a temperature.

Oxide of Barium.—*Baryta*, Ba O, is obtained from the nitrate. It is very similar to lime. Baryta, strontia, lime, and magnesia are distinguished as the "alkaline earths."

Salts of Baryta.—*Nitrate of Baryta*, Ba O, N O_5, is prepared by dissolving the carbonate in nitric acid.

Sulphate of Baryta, Ba O, S O_3, is the white and highly insoluble precipitate which falls whenever a solution containing sulphuric acid is presented to a compound of barium. It is sometimes used as a paint under the name of permanent white.

Other Compounds of Barium.—*Chloride of Barium*, Ba Cl, as well as nitrate of baryta, is used as a test for sulphuric acid, with which it forms a white precipitate of sulphate of baryta.

Barium compounds impart a green colour to flame.

STRONTIUM, Sr = 43·8.

Strontium is in all respects very like barium. It is the basis of the alkaline earth strontia. I have already mentioned (v. page 144) the only fact about strontium which possesses much interest, viz., its property of communicating a red colour to flame. Nitrate of strontia ($Sr O, N O_5$) is largely prepared for this purpose.

The sulphate of strontia differs from the sulphate of baryta in being very slightly soluble in water.

CALCIUM, Ca = 20.

This metal, which is prepared with great difficulty by a process similar to that by which barium and strontium are obtained, is chiefly interesting from its being the basis of the highly important substance, *lime*.

Oxide of Calcium.—*Lime*, Ca O.—I need say no more of the importance of this oxide than to tell you that it forms more than half of both chalk and marble, that it is the base of plaster-of-paris and alabaster; and that with phosphoric acid it constitutes the chief part of the bones of animals.

Anhydrous lime, or "quick-lime," as it is usually called, is prepared by heating common chalk in lime-kilns. These are merely furnaces in which the lime, mixed with fuel, is exposed to a high temperature in the open air. Chalk is a *carbonate* of lime, and the heat drives the carbonic acid off into the air, leaving the lime behind. The escape of carbonic acid is the cause of the disagreeable and suffocating fumes which issue from lime-kilns.

Quick-lime is a highly caustic and powerful base. Like potash, it has a very strong affinity for water. When a little water is sprinkled on quick-lime, it is absorbed, and much heat is given out during the process: *hydrate of lime*, $Ca\,O, H\,O$, or "slaked lime," as it is often called, being produced. To prove the heat given out by lime in "slaking," or combining with water, put a little quick-lime in a heap on a board, and place a small piece of phosphorus on the top. Moisten the bottom of the heap with water, and let it spread through the lime. The heat given out will ignite the phosphorus. Under the most favourable circumstances, enough heat is said to be evolved to char wood. Hydrate of lime is slightly soluble in water, the solution is the lime-water which I have previously mentioned as being a test for carbonic acid (page 36).

Salts of Lime.—Carbonate of Lime, $Ca\,O, C\,O_2$, you already know something about. It enters into a great variety of shapes, constituting, besides chalk and marble, the beautiful calcareous spar found in Derbyshire and other places, and several other minerals.

Sulphate of Lime, $Ca\,O, S\,O_3$, is also a very important salt, inasmuch as it constitutes "plaster-of-paris." This substance is nearly anhydrous, and when it is mixed with water it combines with a portion of it, forming a compound which has that curious property of "setting" into hardness, which renders it so valuable in the arts.

Other Compounds of Calcium.—Of these, *chloride of calcium*, $Ca\,Cl$, is by far the most important. It is very deliquescent, absorbing water with eagerness, and on this account it is much used in chemistry for the purpose of drying gases. The salt is placed in a tube, through which the gas to be dried is made to pass.

Magnesium, Mg = 12.

When sodium is heated in a tube with an excess of chloride of magnesium, metallic magnesium remains in the tube, and if the excess of the materials be removed by water, will be obtained pure. It is a white, malleable metal, fusible below a red heat, and very volatile. It burns very beautifully in oxygen gas, and even in the flame of a common spirit-lamp, giving a flame of extraordinary brilliancy, and producing magnesia.

Magnesia.—Calcined Magnesia, Mg O.—This may be obtained by heating the common *magnesia alba* of commerce, which is a compound of the hydrate and carbonate, to bright redness. It is very feebly soluble in water.

Salts of Magnesia.—The most important is the sulphate, $Mg\,O, S\,O_3$, which is commonly known as "Epsom salts." It is found in many mineral waters, and also in sea water. It is generally prepared from a stone called dolomite, or magnesian limestone.

Other compounds of Magnesium.—The *chloride*, Mg Cl, is formed when magnesia is dissolved in hydrochloric acid. When the solution is evaporated, however, double decomposition takes place between the salt and a portion of the water; hydrochloric acid is given off, and common magnesia remains:—

$$Mg\,Cl + H\,O = Mg\,O + H\,Cl.$$

The salt may however be obtained anhydrous by

mixing its solution with solution of chloride of ammonium, evaporating to dryness and igniting. Its chief use is for the preparation of the metal.

ALUMINUM, Al = 13·7.

This metal, although till very lately it was scarcely known in a separate state, is of the highest importance, from the great abundance of its oxide, alumina. M. Deville, who has the direction of the private laboratory of the Emperor of the French, has within the last few years discovered a process by which the metal may be obtained in large quantities, and at as low a price as silver. The same chemist has made us acquainted with a great many interesting properties possessed by it. It is a white metal, closely resembling silver in its colour and hardness, as well as in its power of resisting the action of air and water, but differing very remarkably from it in weight, silver being four times heavier than aluminum. The consequence of this is, that articles can be made of this new and very beautiful metal for one fourth of the cost of silver. It has already been employed to a considerable extent for ornamental purposes. Deville's process for obtaining it consists of acting on the chloride of aluminum, first by sodium, and afterwards by hydrogen. Aluminum burns very beautifully in oxygen gas, producing alumina.

Sesquioxide of Aluminum.—Alumina, Al_2O_3.—This, the only known oxide, is the representative of a class of metallic oxides called *earths*. With the exception of alumina, they are all very rare. Alumina is found in nature in a great variety of forms and in immense quantities. The *corundum, sapphire*, and *ruby*, besides common *emery*, and some other minerals, are almost pure alumina, while in combination with silicic acid it forms a large part of felspar (one of the constituents of granite), porphyry, garnet, topaz, and an almost infinite number of other minerals, and above all of the various kinds of common clay. It takes its name from alum, which is one of its most important salts.

Alumina may be obtained as hydrate, $Al_2O_3, 3HO$, by adding excess of ammonia to any of its soluble salts—common alum, for instance. In this state it is a white, semi-transparent, and jelly-like mass, which is soluble in potash, and also in mineral acids. When this is exposed to a high temperature it parts with its water, and is then nearly insoluble.

Salts of Alumina.—With the exception of the silicates, *alum* is by far the most important salt of alumina. It is a *double salt*, that is, a compound of two salts together, and its crystals contain twenty-four equivalents of water of crystallization, so that the following is the formula for the salt:—

$$KO, SO_3 + Al_2O_3, 3SO_3 + 24HO.$$

You see the two salts are sulphate of potash and sulphate of alumina. There are a great many other salts similarly constituted. The twenty-four equivalents of water may all be expelled by a very moderate heat. Alum is used in immense quantities by dyers and calico printers.

The *silicate* of alumina, as I have before mentioned, constitutes the main part of the various kinds of clay which are used for the manufacture of bricks, pottery, and porcelain.

CHAPTER XI.

METALS—*continued.*

CLASS II.

Metals proper, fusible below a red heat.

LEAD, Pb = 103.

THIS useful metal is found in great abundance in the British islands, no less than 63,999 tons having been extracted in the year 1854; 322 mines being at that time worked. It very seldom occurs native, but nearly always in combination with sulphur, as *sulphide of lead,* the common lead-ore which is called "galena" by mineralogists. The metal is obtained from this ore by a process which consists of two stages, the first being what is called "roasting." This consists in heating it in a peculiarly constructed furnace, in the presence of air. The roasting converts the ore into a mixture of *sulphate of lead* ($Pb\,O, S\,O_3$) and sulphide of lead ($Pb\,S$). This mixture is then exposed to a stronger heat, when metallic lead is left behind, and sulphurous acid gas passes off:—

$$Pb\,O, S\,O_3 + Pb\,S = 2\,Pb + 2\,S\,O_2.$$

The English lead-mines have been of importance ever since the time of the Romans. There are in the

British Museum some "pigs," or bars of lead, which were found in various parts of England, and which are marked with the names of the Emperors Domitian, Hadrian, and Vespasian. Pliny says that in his time the British lead-mines were very large. Lead is a soft, bluish-grey, and very heavy metal. It speedily tarnishes when exposed to the air. Lead is used for a great variety of purposes in the arts. One of its most curious applications is for the manufacture of *shot*. These are made by pouring the melted metal from the top of a high tower into water. During its descent it congeals into round globules. This process was first discovered by a workman named Watt, who is said to have thought of it in a dream. He went next morning to the top of the church of St. Mary Redcliffe, at Bristol, where he lived, and tried the experiment, which, to his surprise, succeeded. When first separated from the ore, lead always contains more or less silver. This can be extracted from it by a very interesting process, and it is occasionally present in such quantities as to be worth more than the lead which contained it. In 1854, 562,659 ounces of silver were obtained from English lead.

Oxides of Lead.—

Suboxide of lead	Pb_2O.
Protoxide of lead (litharge) .	PbO.
Binoxide of lead	PbO_2.

Red lead is a compound of the two last oxides.

Of these oxides the protoxide, or litharge, is the most important. You can prepare this in the following manner:—

Take a solution of nitrate of lead, and pour into it a solution of ammonia, until it is strongly ammoniacal. A white precipitate will fall. This precipitate is *hydrated oxide of lead*, Pb O, H O.

Prepare a paper filter (fig. 27), put it on a funnel with a glass beneath, and pour the ammoniacal liquid, precipitate and all, on to the filter. There is a very convenient plan in use among chemists for pouring from basins and glasses, on to filters. Every glass vessel and basin which contains a liquid, should have a glass stirring-rod in it. This is merely a piece of glass rod a little longer than the basin is wide (fig.

Fig. 40.

40). It may be cut from a longer piece with a file like glass tubing, and the ends rounded in the flame of a spirit-lamp.

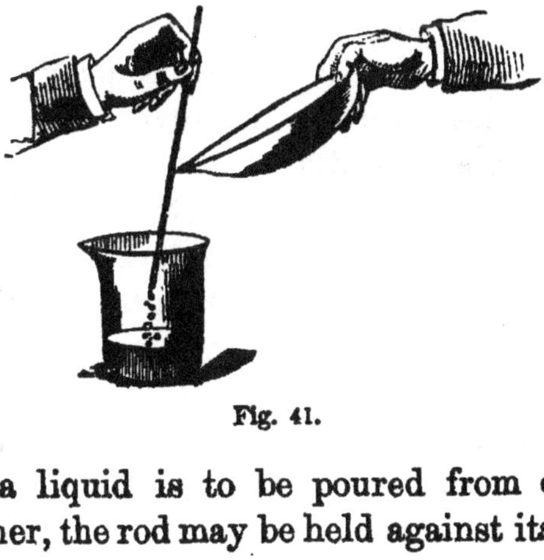

Fig. 41.

When a liquid is to be poured from one vessel into another, the rod may be held against its edge, and the liquid allowed to run down it. Not a drop will be lost, if the transference be neatly made.

In this way you are to transfer the hydrated oxide of lead on to the filter you have prepared. It is nearly insoluble in water, and therefore will not pass through the filter. The next thing is to *wash* it, so as to separate it from the solution by which it is accompanied. This requires the aid of a *wash-bottle*, a piece of apparatus which is constantly wanted, and which I therefore give a drawing of. A strong, flat-bottomed flask

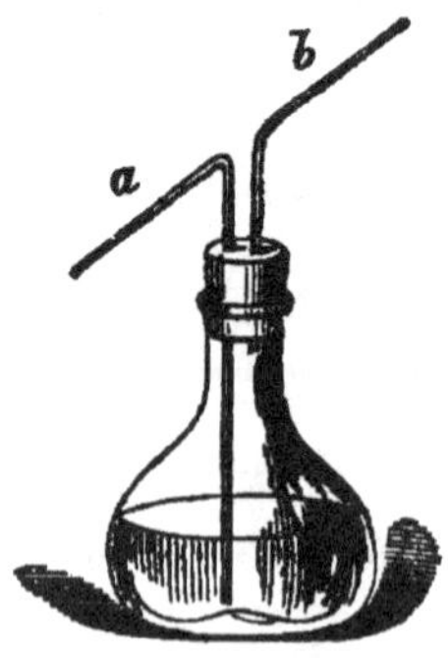

Fig. 42.

is chosen, and fitted with two tubes passing through a cork. Of these *a* goes right down to the bottom of the flask, and at the other end is drawn out to a fine jet. The other one, *b*, only just passes through the cork. When the flask contains water, a fine stream of it can be directed through *a* on any required object by blowing through *b*. The whole apparatus may be put over a lamp and the water boiled. Hot water is very frequently required.

Well, to return to the experiment before us, the wash-bottle being filled with boiling distilled water, direct a stream of it on the filter, and continue to do so until the water rises nearly to the edge of the paper; then let it stand until all the water has run through. When this is the case, fill it up again with hot water, and repeat this process three or four times. The precipitate will then be thoroughly washed. It must next be *dried.* This is done by putting the funnel—filter, precipitate and all, into a basin, resting this basin on a sand-bath, and applying a gentle heat until the paper and the precipitate it contains appear quite dry. The precipitate may then be removed from the filter.

I have described these details very minutely because they are of constant occurrence and immense importance, especially in the department of *analytical* chemistry. Upon the neatness and accuracy with which they are done, depends the success of a host of operations, and you cannot, therefore, pay too much attention to them.

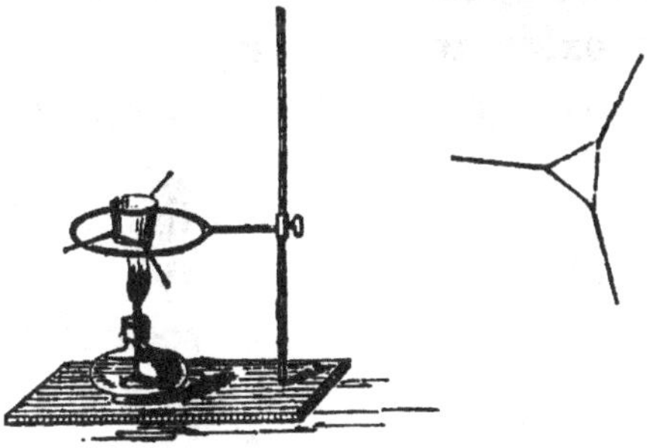

Fig. 43.

The dry hydrate is to be put into a small porcelain crucible, and supported over a lamp, on a triangle made of twisted iron wire.

When it has been heated some time, it assumes a red colour. When this is the case, you may be sure that the water is all expelled, and may remove the lamp, and allow the oxide of lead to cool.

The following is the explanation of the process by which you obtained it:—

Nitrate of Oxide of Lead.	Ammonia. Water.	Hydrate of Oxide of Lead.	Nitrate of Ammonia.

$$PbO, NO_5 + NH_4O, HO = PbO, HO + NH_4O, NO_5.$$

And on heating the hydrate—

$$PbO, HO = PbO + HO.$$

Salts of Protoxide of Lead.—These are very numerous. The most important are the acetate and the carbonate. You may obtain the *nitrate* (PbO, NO_5) by dissolving the protoxide of lead in dilute nitric acid, and evaporating the solution to a small bulk, when white crystals form on cooling.

Acetate of Lead, $PbO, \bar{A}$.—The highly poisonous salt, commonly known as "sugar of lead," from its appearance and sweet taste, may be obtained by dissolving the oxide in *acetic acid*, which is the acid contained in vinegar. It is of immense use in the arts.

Carbonate of Lead, PbO, CO_2, the substance called "white lead" by painters, may be prepared by adding solution of carbonate of soda to a solution of nitrate or acetate of lead, and collecting the precipitate on a filter, and washing it:—

Nitrate of Lead.	Carbonate of Soda.	Carbonate of Lead.	Nitrate of Soda.

$$PbO, NO_5 + NaO, CO_2 = PbO, CO_2 + NaO, NO_5.$$

It is a white, insoluble powder, and a deadly poison.

Red Lead, $2\,PbO + PbO_2 = Pb_3O_4$.—I have already told you that this is a compound of two other oxides. It is prepared by exposing the protoxide to a long-continued heat in the air. It is largely used as a paint. The other oxides of lead are unimportant.

Other compounds of Lead.—The *sulphide* I have already alluded to, as the ore from which the metal is obtained. The *chloride*, *iodide*, and *bromide* of lead are of little consequence.

TIN, Sn = 59.

The very earliest records of our island which have been preserved to us, are connected with the working of this metal. It is certain that the ancient Phœnicians, at an extremely remote period, were in the habit of coming over here to dig for tin, and it is for this reason that Herodotus, when he alludes to the "Cassiterides," or tin-islands (*cassiteros*, tin), is generally supposed to mean Britain and the Scilly islands.

Cornwall, which has always yielded the chief supply of the metal, abounds with the remains of the old Phœnician, and later Roman workings. The metal is most commonly found in the state of oxide, from which it is obtained by roasting and subsequent reduction by fusion with coal. It is brought to market in two shapes, distinguished as "grain-tin" and "bar-tin," of which the former, which is obtained from ore found in the soft beds of rivers, is the best.

Tin is a white, and very bright metal. It is malleable, and may be beaten out into thin plates, which are known as tin-foil. At ordinary temperatures, tin is but very slowly tarnished by contact with moist air, and it is to this circumstance that its principal use in the arts is owing. Every one knows that what is called "tin-plate," is not really tin, but only iron coated over with that metal.

Iron, as you know, is so easily oxidized, that saucepans and other utensils made of it, and not covered with anything else, would soon become covered with rust, and wear into holes. To avoid this, the iron is made perfectly clean, and dipped into melted tin, with many precautions. The tin adheres to the iron, and effectually protects it from rusting. This process is called "tinning," and is applied to copper as well as iron. In the case of copper, it is peculiarly important, because copper-rust, which usually consists of carbonate, is highly poisonous.

Tin melts at a low temperature for a metal, but it does not, like zinc and some others, volatilize or rise in vapour. When heated to a high temperature in the air, it burns with a beautiful white light, yielding binoxide of tin.

When a bar of tin is bent, it emits a curious crackling sound, and if this be repeated two or three times, the bar becomes sensibly hot.

Hydrochloric acid dissolves tin with the aid of heat, though rather slowly; protochloride of tin being formed. Nitric acid attacks it energetically, but instead of dissolving it, converts it into a white powder (metastannic acid).

Oxides of Tin.—

Protoxide of tin	$Sn\,O$.
Binoxide of tin	$Sn\,O_2$.

The former of these may be obtained as a white insoluble hydrate, $Sn\,O, H\,O$, by precipitating a solution of the protochloride with carbonate of potash or soda. It loses its water when heated.

When the anhydrous oxide is heated in the air, it glows, and is converted into the binoxide. It is a weak base. Its salts are of little importance.

Binoxide of Tin is interesting in a chemical point of view from the fact that it exists in combination with water, in two distinct forms, both of which possess acid properties. One of these is called *stannic acid*, $H\,O, Sn\,O_2$, while the other, which is known as *metastannic acid*, possesses the curious formula $10\,H\,O, Sn_5\,O_{10}$. Each of these hydrated acids gives rise to a distinct class of salts, distinguished as the *stannates* and the *metastannates*.

Other compounds of Tin.—These are two chlorides of tin, both of them very important compounds.

Protochloride of Tin, $Sn\,Cl$, may be obtained by dissolving tin in boiling hydrochloric acid, and crystallising the salt out. It forms colourless, transparent crystals.

Bichloride of Tin, $Sn\,Cl_2$, is a curious colourless, and volatile liquid, which fumes in the air. Both these chlorides of tin are of great importance to the dyer and calico printer.

The substance called mosaic gold is a *bisulphide of tin* ($Sn\,S_2$).

When a piece of zinc is immersed in a solution containing tin, the protochloride for instance, the tin is deposited on its surface in the same manner as the lead in the "lead tree" (v. page 21).

Arsenic, As = 75.

This metal possesses a high degree of interest for us, from the deadly nature of its compounds. It is found in small quantities in a great many minerals, but the chief supply of it is obtained from Silesia, where a native arsenical sulphide of iron, called mispickel, is found in abundance.

Arsenic is a bright, steel-grey metal, very brittle and very fusible. It is so volatile that it may be sublimed like sulphur.

Oxides of Arsenic.—Arsenic forms two compounds with oxygen, both of them acids.

Arsenious acid	$As\,O_3$.
Arsenic acid	$As\,O_5$.

Arsenious Acid is the substance sold in the shops as *white arsenic*, or sometimes simply as arsenic. It is sparingly soluble in water, and gives rise to a class of salts called *arsenites*. It is one of the most deadly poisons known.

Arsenic Acid is obtained from the preceding oxide. It bears a close analogy to tribasic phosphoric acid. It is even more poisonous than arsenious acid.

Other Compounds of Arsenic.—Arsenic forms several compounds with sulphur. Of these the *tersulphide*, $As\,S_3$, which constitutes the colour called *orpiment*, and which is the chief ingredient in the paint sold as "King's yellow," is the most important.

Arsenic combines with hydrogen, and forms with it a gas to which I shall allude again very soon. It is called *arseniuretted hydrogen*, and has a similar composition to phosphoretted hydrogen, AsH_3. It burns with a blue flame, producing water and arsenious acid. If any cold body be introduced into this flame, the arsenic will be deposited in a metallic state upon it.

Tests for Arsenic.—The compounds of arsenic are so intensely poisonous, and one of them, arsenious acid, has, unfortunately, been the occasion of so many fatal accidents, and the instrument of so many secret murders, that it is of the highest importance that the chemist should be in possession of accurate tests by which to ascertain the presence or absence of the metal. To show the delicacy necessary for this purpose, I may mention that it is considered that under certain circumstances *three grains* of arsenious acid may cause death.

I have purposely avoided giving you any experiments with this metal, on account of the great danger which attends working with it, but the one which I am about to describe is quite safe.

Fit a small flask or bottle with a cork, and a jet of glass tube passing through it. Nearly all the common zinc of commerce contains small quantities of arsenic, and it is this arsenic which I wish you to detect. Into the flask or bottle put a few pieces of common zinc, and pour a little water on it; then add a small quantity of hydrochloric acid, and replace the cork and jet. Hydrogen gas will, as you already know, be evolved. When you think the common air is expelled, light the gas at the jet. Now, when hydrogen gas is set free in the presence of arsenic, it combines with it and forms arseniuretted hydrogen, so that if arsenic was present in the zinc, the flame which is now burning, will contain it. To ascertain this point, take the white porcelain cover of a crucible, and depress it for an instant on the flame, in the manner shown in fig. 44.

Fig. 44.

If there was the smallest trace of arsenic in the zinc, a black stain of metallic arsenic will be left on the porcelain. This test alone, however, is not quite conclusive, for it happens that antimony forms a similar compound with hydrogen, and is deposited in a precisely similar manner on a plate. How then are we to discriminate between the two? Very simply.

Dissolve a little *chloride of lime*, or bleaching powder, in water, and pour a few drops of the solution on the stain on the porcelain. If the stain be arsenic it will instantly dissolve, while if it consist of antimony it will remain unchanged. This test, by means of hydrogen, is known as "Marsh's test," from the name of its discoverer, and is amazingly accurate. If by any chance the zinc should be free from both arsenic and antimony, you may dissolve a few *shot*, which nearly always contain the former metal, in a little dilute nitric acid, and add some of this solution to the zinc and hydrochloric acid.

ANTIMONY, Sb = 120·6.

Antimony presents a very close resemblance to arsenic in its general characters. It is nearly always found in the state of sulphide, from which it is obtained by roasting and subsequent reduction by fusion with charcoal and carbonate of soda. It is a white, brittle metal, which may be readily fused, and, with some difficulty, volatilized. At ordinary temperatures it is not acted on by moist or dry air; but when heated in the air, it burns with a white flame, and copious fumes of teroxide. Some of the alloys of antimony are valuable: "type metal" and "Britannia metal" both contain a good deal of it. Nitric acid converts it into a white, insoluble powder, antimonic acid. Hydrochloric acid and nitro-hydrochloric acid dissolve it.

Oxides of Antimony.—

Teroxide of antimony . . . . $Sb\,O_3$.
Antimonic acid . . . . . . $Sb\,O_5$.

Besides an intermediate oxide.

The *teroxide* may be obtained by throwing the terchloride into a solution of carbonate of soda. It is a white powder, and forms a class of salts, most of which possess the curious property of decomposing when thrown into water. *Tartar emetic*, which is an important exception to this rule, is a tartrate of potash and teroxide of antimony.

$$K\,O,\ Sb\,O_3,\ \bar{T}.$$

It is largely used in medicine as an emetic.

Antimonic Acid is produced by action of nitric acid on antimony. It is a weak acid.

Other Compounds of Antimony.—The *terchloride*, $SbCl_3$, is the white solid produced when powdered antimony was inflamed by sprinkling it in chlorine (v. page 91). It may also be obtained in solution by dissolving common sulphide of antimony, in strong boiling hydrochloric acid:—

$$Sb\,S_3 + 3\,H\,Cl = Sb\,Cl_3 + 3\,H\,S.$$

Hydrosulphuric acid is set free, and a solution obtained which, when thrown into water, gives a white precipitate.

The *tersulphide*, $Sb\,S_3$, the most important of the sulphides, I have already mentioned as being found native. In that form it is a black substance with a metallic lustre like lead. When prepared by adding hydrosulphuric acid to a solution of antimony (page 105), it is an orange-coloured powder. This curious difference of colour in the same substance has been the occasion of a good deal of speculation.

Bismuth, Bi = 213.

This metal in many respects resembles the last. It is white, brittle, and easily fusible, and may be obtained in beautiful crystals.

Melt some of the metal in a small earthen crucible, allow it to cool till a crust has formed on its surface, then pierce this crust with a wire, and pour the melted metal out through it. When cold the crucible may be broken, and a beautiful mass of hollow cubical crystals will be found within.

Bismuth forms many alloys. The most curious of them is that called "fusible metal." This is obtained by heating together two parts of bismuth, one of lead, and one of tin. This mixture actually fuses below the temperature of boiling water, so that a spoon made of it would melt in a cup of boiling hot tea. The compounds of bismuth are but of slight interest. Several of its salts throw down a white precipitate when mixed with water, in the same manner as the salts of antimony.

ZINC, Zn = 32·6.

Comparatively little of this valuable metal is found in our own country, the principal part of our supply being obtained from Siberia and Belgium. It is most often found in the form of carbonate or sulphide. The ore after being roasted—a process which converts it into oxide—is mixed with powdered coke, and heated strongly in large iron crucibles, so constructed that the volatile metal may distil over in a state of comparative purity.

Zinc is a hard, bluish-white metal, which is rather brittle at ordinary temperatures, but, when heated to a certain degree, becomes quite malleable, and may be rolled into plates or otherwise worked.

Zinc is used for a number of useful purposes, among

which I may particularly mention the manufacture of "galvanized iron," as it is called, and which consists of iron coated with zinc in the same manner as with tin. Zinc forms several valuable alloys.

Oxide of Zinc, Zn O.—This, which is the only known oxide, is produced when zinc is heated strongly in the air.

Under the head of oxygen (page 41), I described an experiment by which zinc may be burnt in an iron ladle. The white fumes which rise in such abundance during that experiment consist of oxide. You may burn thin shreds of zinc, and show the beautiful green light which it gives, by holding them in the flame of hydrogen. Oxide of zinc may likewise be prepared by precipitating a salt of zinc by a slight excess of potash or soda, and heating the precipitate. It is yellow while hot, but gets white on cooling. It is now used largely as a substitute for white-lead.

Salts of Zinc.—The *sulphate*, ZnO, SO_3, which is the most important, may be obtained by dissolving the metal in dilute sulphuric acid, as in the process for preparing hydrogen. It forms colourless crystals—the "white-vitriol" of commerce.

Other Compounds of Zinc.—*Chloride of Zinc*, Zn Cl, is obtained by dissolving the metal in hydrochloric acid. It is very soluble in water, and, when anhydrous, highly corrosive to the skin.

Mercury, or Quicksilver, Hg = 100.

Like the preceding metal, mercury is nearly always found in the state of sulphide. The ore is called "cinnabar." There are quicksilver mines in several parts of the world; Austria, California, and Australia containing very important ores. But by far the oldest, the largest, and the most celebrated, are those at Almaden in Spain, where there is a small hill which contains an enormous quantity of cinnabar. Theophrastus, who lived 300 years before Christ, alludes to these mines as being then worked, and Pliny tells us that the Greeks obtained their supply from them as long ago as 700 B.C. In his time the mine was kept sealed with the greatest care, and never opened except to take out the quantity necessary for the consumption of Rome.

In 1833, when a French geologist visited Almaden, 700 men were employed under ground, and 200 more on the surface, and the quantity of mercury produced amounted to 2,244,000 lbs. a year. The deleterious fumes of the metal are said to have a dreadful effect on the health of the men employed in working the ore, though with proper care this might in great measure be avoided.

There are several processes by which the metal can be obtained from cinnabar. One is to heat the ore in large furnaces with a limited supply of air. The sulphur is converted into sulphurous acid, which is given off as gas, as in the case of lead; while the mercury, being volatile, passes off with it, and is condensed in a suitable chamber. Mercury is always conveyed in iron bottles, which hold seventy-five pounds each.

Mercury is a silver-white, and very bright metal. Unlike all other metals, it is a liquid at ordinary temperatures. When cooled, however, to 40° below zero it becomes solid, and is then soft and malleable, and in all respects like any other metal. In fact, we ought to consider mercury as a metal which melts at a very low temperature, though it appears to our notions rather strange that a melted metal should afford no sensation of heat to our bodies.

Mercury is a very heavy metal: it is thirteen times heavier than water, and when in the solid state, it is still heavier. When heated strongly it boils, and rises in colourless and invisible vapour, and for this reason may be distilled. In fact, the distillation of mercury is a very common process, as it affords a convenient means of separating it from other metals. Mercury is much used for the manufacture of thermometers and barometers, and also for the "silvering," as it is incorrectly called, of looking-glasses. This last process is performed with an amalgam of mercury and tin. I have already told you that the alloys of mercury with other metals are called amalgams.

Oxides of Mercury.—

Suboxide of mercury, $Hg_2 O$.
Protoxide of mercury, $Hg O$ (often called peroxide).

The first of these oxides may be prepared by precipitating a solution of subnitrate of mercury ($Hg_2 O, N O_5$) by excess of potash. It is a dark-grey powder, and is the base of a class of salts called the "subsalts of mercury."

The protoxide of mercury may be obtained by precipitating the protonitrate ($Hg O, N O_5$) by potash, in the same way as for the suboxide. When prepared in this way, it is a bright-yellow powder, but when prepared, as it often is, by decomposing either of the nitrates by heat, it has a fine red colour. It parts with its oxygen on exposure to heat (v. page 27). Protoxide of mercury is, like the suboxide, the base of a class of salts known as the "protosalts," or the "per-salts" (it being the highest known oxide), of mercury.

Salts of the Oxides of Mercury.—The most important of these are the two nitrates before alluded to. They may be thus prepared :—

1. *Subnitrate of Mercury*, Hg_2O, NO_5.—Dissolve a globule of mercury in cold dilute nitric acid. The solution will contain the salt, which may be separated by crystallization.

2. *Protonitrate of Mercury*, HgO, NO_5.—Instead of the metal, dissolve protoxide of mercury in nitric acid. In this case you will not be able to crystallize out the salt, as it can only be done with difficulty, you must be satisfied with a solution of it.

Other Compounds of Mercury.—There are two very important chlorides of mercury.

Subchloride of mercury, Hg_2Cl.—Calomel.

Protochloride of mercury, $HgCl$.—Corrosive sublimate (often called perchloride).

Calomel may be prepared by adding a solution of common salt to a solution of subnitrate of mercury, when it falls as a white insoluble powder. Nitrate of soda is left in solution :—

$$Hg_2O, NO_5 + NaCl = Hg_2Cl + NaO, NO_5.$$

Corrosive Sublimate may be obtained by dissolving the

protoxide in hot hydrochloric acid, when crystals will separate on cooling. Both these chlorides, the former especially, are of great use in medicine. Corrosive sublimate is one of the most deadly poisons known.

Sulphide of Mercury, Hg S.—Take six parts of mercury and one of sulphur. Melt the sulphur in a crucible, throw the mercury into it, and stir the whole for some time. A blackish-red mass will be produced. Take a little of this, and heat it in a dry test-tube. A beautiful red powder, known as *vermilion*, will sublime and deposit itself on the sides of the tube. Both the brownish-red mass and the bright-red powder have the same composition, Hg S, they only differ in shape. None of the other compounds of mercury are of any great importance.

Test for Mercury.—Take any solution containing mercury, immerse in it a few slips of bright copper, and heat them together in a test-tube. The copper will be coated with a bright deposit of metallic mercury. Take the copper so coated, out, dry it carefully with blotting-paper, and put it into a clean and dry test-tube. Heat it gently over a spirit-lamp, when the mercury will leave the copper of its original colour, and settle in minute globules on the sides of the tube, where it will be very apparent if the inside of the tube be scraped with a glass rod.

Class III.

Metals proper, infusible below a Red-heat.

Iron, Fe = 28.

Of all the metals which contribute to the service of man, none is so important, or so varied in its uses as iron; and this is the more fortunate because it is found in much larger quantity than any other. We may well take pride also, as Englishmen, in the thought that no other country approaches our own in the amount of this treasure which it supplies.

The following table, showing in round numbers the estimated quantity of the metal produced in the year 1854, will illustrate this:—

From the mines of—	Tons.
Staffordshire, were produced .	847,000
Other counties in England . .	643,000
Wales	783,000
Scotland	796,000
Total in Great Britain . .	3,069,000
From all other countries in the world put together	3,000,000
Total produce	6,069,000

You see that Great Britain produced more than all the other countries in the world put together.

There are many different ores of iron, but the most important consist of the carbonate, and the various kinds of oxide. These are smelted in very large furnaces, fifty feet or more in height, with a mixture of coke and limestone, and the melted metal which collects at the bottom is drawn off into narrow troughs made in sand. Here it cools into bars of cast iron, which are called "pigs." The pigs are subsequently re-melted in smaller furnaces, and cast into moulds of any required form.

Wrought Iron, or malleable iron, is prepared by a

curious process which is called "puddling," and which you will find described in all books on metallurgy.

Oxides of Iron.—These are four in number, but the most important are the two following, both of them bases:—

Protoxide of Iron, $Fe\,O$.
Sesquioxide of iron, $Fe_2\,O_3$.

Like the oxides of mercury and lead, these two oxides gives rise to different and quite dissimilar classes of salts, the first being distinguished as the "proto-salts," and the other as the "sesqui-salts," or "per-salts" of iron.

Protoxide of Iron.—If you add to a solution of proto-sulphate of iron (green vitriol), a solution of ammonia, a precipitate will be produced, which at first will be almost white, but will speedily change to a dirty-green, and at last to a sort of reddish brown.

The precipitate at first produced, consisted principally of hydrated protoxide of iron. I say principally, because there is almost always a small proportion of sesquioxide with it; were it not so, the precipitate would be white. This protoxide of iron has such an affinity for oxygen that even in a few minutes it absorbs it, and is gradually converted into the sesquioxide.

Sesquioxide of Iron.—If you add ammonia to a per-salt of iron, such for instance as the sesquisulphate, instead of the greenish-white precipitate produced in the previous case, a reddish-brown one will be formed. This is the hydrated sesquioxide of iron, $Fe_2\,O_3$, $3\,H\,O$, and if it be dried over a lamp, anhydrous oxide will remain. It is the same as common red rust, which is produced when iron is exposed to moist air.

Salts of the Oxides of Iron.—The most important are the two sulphates to which I have already alluded.

The *protosulphate*, $Fe\,O, S\,O_3$, which is often called green vitriol, or "copperas," may be obtained by dissolving iron in dilute sulphuric acid. Hydrogen gas is given off during the process:—

$$Fe + H\,O, S\,O_3 = Fe\,O, S\,O_3 + H.$$

Beautiful green crystals of the salt are formed one vaporation, which contain seven equivalents of water.

The sesquisulphate may be procured either by dissolving the sesquioxide in sulphuric acid, or by adding nitric acid, a few drops at a time, to a solution of the protosulphate until no more red fumes are given off. The small excess of nitric acid may then be got rid of, by boiling the solution for some time. It does not crystallize.

Other compounds of Iron.—There are two chlorides of iron, the *protochloride*, $Fe\,Cl$, and the *sesquichloride*, $Fe_2\,Cl_3$. These may be obtained in exactly the same manner as the sulphates, using hydrochloric acid instead of sulphuric. There are likewise two sulphides.

Tests for Iron.—*Ferrocyanide of potassium* gives a beautiful blue precipitate of Prussian blue, with per-salts of iron. With proto-salts it gives a pale-blue precipitate, which becomes darker on exposure to the air.

Sulphocyanide of potassium gives with per-salts of iron

a blood-red colour, but no precipitate. This colour is so like blood that it is sometimes used on the stage to represent it. If you moisten your hand with solution of sulphocyanide of potassium, and then dipping a knife in a solution of a per-salt of iron (say the sesquisulphate or sesquichloride), touch the hand with it, pretending to cut it, you will see how perfect the deception is. Any one would imagine that you had made a dreadful gash in your hand.

Tincture of gall-nuts, added to a per-salt of iron, produces an intense bluish-black colour, which is that to which common ink owes its blackness.

MANGANESE, Mn = 27·6.

The most important ore of this metal, the black oxide, or binoxide, is found in considerable quantities, and is an important article of trade. The metal is obtained from it by a somewhat difficult process, which however depends on its reduction by fusion with charcoal.

The properties of manganese are remarkable. It is greyish-white in colour, with a faint tinge of red. It is very brittle, but so exceedingly hard that it will scratch the hardest steel, and will scratch and even cut glass. Manganese readily decomposes water—when in a state of powder, even at the lowest temperatures. It dissolves rapidly in dilute sulphuric acid. When a very small quantity of manganese is alloyed with iron, the quality of the latter is said to be much improved by it.

Oxides of Manganese.—No fewer than seven of these have been discovered, but of this number two appear to be compounds of other oxides with one another. They present the unusual case of a series of oxides, containing bases, neutral bodies, and acids, in their number.

Protoxide	$Mn\,O$—Basic.
Sesquioxide	$Mn_2\,O_3$—Basic.
Binoxide	$Mn\,O_2$—Neutral.
Manganic acid	$Mn\,O_3$—Acid.
Permanganic acid . .	$Mn_2\,O_7$—Acid.

Protoxide of Manganese.—When ammonia is added to a solution of sulphate of manganese, a white precipitate falls, consisting of hydrated protoxide of manganese, $Mn\,O, H\,O$. This, like the corresponding oxide of iron, speedily becomes brown by absorbing oxygen from the air.

The *protosulphate*, $Mn\,O, S\,O_3$, may be obtained by heating together binoxide of manganese and sulphuric acid. Oxygen escapes during the process:—

$$Mn\,O_2 + H\,O, S\,O_3 = Mn\,O, S\,O_3 + H\,O + O.$$

It is a beautiful rose-coloured, and very soluble salt, and is used in dyeing.

Sesquioxide of Manganese is a weak base, and is produced when the hydrated protoxide is exposed to air.

Binoxide of Manganese I have already told you is found native. When it is heated in an iron retort, oxygen is given off, and a mixture of protoxide and sesquioxide remains:—

$$3\,Mn\,O_2 = Mn_2\,O_3 + Mn\,O + 2\,O.$$

This is the cheapest, though not the most convenient process for preparing oxygen. This oxide is also largely used for making chlorine (v. page 89), and likewise for imparting an amethyst-blue colour to glass.

Manganic and Permanganic Acids.—These two acids are extremely difficult to prepare, and in fact the former has never yet been obtained in a perfectly free state. Their potash salts are the only ones of interest.

Mineral Chameleon, or Manganate of potash.—To prepare this curious salt, mix together four parts finely powdered binoxide of manganese, and three and a half parts of chlorate of potash. Then dissolve five parts of potash in a small quantity of water; add this to the above ingredients, and dry and powder the whole. Put the powder into an earthen crucible, and heat it to dull redness for an hour in a hot fire. When cold, break the crucible, and you will get a green mass. This is manganate of potash. Take a little piece of this green mass, and dissolve it in a very small quantity of water. The solution will have a splendid green colour. Now pour this green solution into a tumbler-full of water, and the colour will instantly change to a bright and very beautiful purple. This curious change is owing to the formation of *permanganate of potash*, which has this fine colour. The other compounds of manganese are unimportant. The beautiful colour which manganese imparts to glass, may be shown by melting a little borax (biborate of soda) in a loop on the end of a platinum wire (fig. 39), and touching the hot bead with a very small quantity of binoxide of manganese. If the bead be now heated strongly in the outer flame of the blowpipe it will assume a beautiful amethyst tint.

CHROMIUM, Cr. = 26·7.

The most important ore of chromium is that known as chrome iron-stone. It can only be reduced with extreme difficulty. When obtained in a fused mass (which can only be effected by the oxy-hydrogen blowpipe), it is stated to be more infusible than platinum, and even harder than manganese. It dissolves readily in hydrochloric acid.

Oxides of Chromium.—The most important are the—

Sesquioxide . . .	$Cr_2 O_3$.
Chromic acid . . .	$Cr O_3$.

Sesquioxide of Chromium.—This oxide may be obtained in a hydrated state, $Cr_2 O_3, 3 H O$, by reducing any soluble chromate.

Take a solution of bichromate of potash, add to it a little sulphuric acid, and heat it in a flask. Then add small successive quantities of common sugar, until a deep-green solution is produced. This solution contains sesqui-sulphate of chromium, $Cr_2 O_3, 3 S O_3$. When this solution is cold, add to it gradually, excess of ammonia. A green precipitate of the hydrated oxide will fall, and may be collected and dried. If ignited, it will lose its water, and become anhydrous.

This experiment is an instructive one, because it affords an instance of the action of a *reducing agent*. The chromic acid in the bichromate of potash loses a part of its oxygen to the sugar, and is reduced to a lower oxide. It is also curious that an acid should so easily become converted into a base.

Another way of forming the anhydrous oxide is the following :—

Mix together, in very fine powder, forty-eight parts of gunpowder, two hundred and forty parts of bichromate of potash, and five parts of chloride of ammonium. Fill a wine-glass with this mixture, press a piece of tin plate on the top of the glass, then invert the whole and remove the wine-glass, leaving the powder in a conical heap on the tin. Apply a light to the top, and it will burn quietly down, leaving a bright-green mass of oxide of chromium. It is used for enamel painting.

Chromic Acid.—This highly important acid can only be obtained in a state of purity with some difficulty. It forms beautiful crimson crystals.

Of the salts of chromic acid, by far the most important is *bichromate of potash*, $KO, 2\,CrO_3$. With this you are already acquainted. *Chromate of lead*, PbO, CrO_3, produced by mixing solutions of bichromate of potash and a salt of lead, is used in painting as "chrome yellow."

COBALT, Co = 29·5.

This is a white, brittle metal, which is strongly magnetic. With iron and nickel, both likewise magnetic, it constitutes the "meteoric iron" which occasionally falls from the sky.

Protoxide of Cobalt, CoO.—The only oxide of importance. It is obtained by precipitating chloride or sulphate of cobalt with carbonate of soda, and washing, drying, and igniting the precipitate. It is a grey powder.

Protoxide of cobalt imparts a beautiful blue colour

to glass. Fuse a very minute quantity with borax, as you did with manganese, and observe the colour. If you use much oxide, the colour will be so deep as to look black. Powdered glasses of this kind, constitute the "smalt" and "cobalt-blue" so much used by painters.

Nitrate of Cobalt, $Co\,O, N\,O_5$, obtained by dissolving the oxide in nitric acid, is a beautiful pink salt.

Take a little solution of this salt, and add ammonia to it, slowly. A fine blue precipitate will be produced, which will dissolve with some difficulty in excess, forming a *brownish-red* solution. This is a very valuable test for cobalt.

Chloride of Cobalt, $Co\,Cl$.—If oxide of cobalt be dissolved in hydrochloric acid, and the solution evaporated, splendid ruby-red crystals of this salt will be obtained.

If these crystals be dissolved in a *small* quantity of water, the solution will be *deep blue*, but if more water be added, it becomes *pink*. This curious property of the salt has caused its employment as a *sympathetic* or invisible ink. Write on paper with a clean quill pen dipped in the dilute solution. The characters will be invisible when dry. But if the paper be held before the fire they will become blue, because a portion of the water they still contained has been driven off. After a short time the colour will fade away, the salt absorbing water from the air, and this may be repeated any number of times.

It is easy to see how a knowledge of this property might be taken advantage of to carry on a secret correspondence.

NICKEL, Ni = 29·6.

Nickel bears a most curious resemblance to the preceding metal in its chemical properties. It is generally found associated with it, in nature.

Protoxide of Nickel, Ni O.—To a solution of sulphate of nickel, add excess of potash. The green precipitate which falls is hydrated oxide, Ni O, H O. When ignited, an ash-grey powder, the anhydrous oxide, is obtained.

The most important salt of this oxide is the sulphate (Ni O, $S O_3$), which has a beautiful green colour. To a solution of this sulphate add ammonia. A beautiful green precipitate is produced, which is soluble in excess, and a fine *blue* solution is produced. This is the best test for nickel.

COPPER, Cu = 31·7.

Copper is found in large quantities in Great Britain, especially in the counties of Cornwall and Devon, in which it is a most important article of trade, some of the mines in those counties being astonishingly remunerative. It is also very abundant in Australia, America, and many other parts of the world. It is sometimes found native, blocks having been occasionally discovered which weighed many tons; but, like lead and mercury, it generally occurs in the state of sulphide. From this it is obtained by a long and rather complicated process.

When pure it is a beautiful red metal, somewhat heavier than iron, but not so heavy as lead. It does not tarnish by exposure to dry air, but in moist air it becomes covered with a green coating of carbonate, by absorbing carbonic acid from the air. It is very malleable and ductile.

Oxides of Copper.—These are two in number, both of them being bases:—

Suboxide of copper . . . Cu_2O.
Protoxide of copper . . . CuO.

The protoxide is by far the most important of these. The black scales which form on the surface of copper, when it is exposed to a red heat in the air, consist of it; but it may be more conveniently prepared by heating the nitrate to redness in a crucible, the acid in this case being dissipated, and the black oxide remaining.

You may prepare a little in the following way:—Take a solution of sulphate of copper, and add to it a slight excess of solution of potash. A pale-blue precipitate will fall (see page 142), consisting of hydrate of the protoxide, CuO, HO. If this blue precipitate be boiled with the liquid which contains it, it gradually becomes black. It is then found to have lost its water, having become converted into the anhydrous oxide, CuO.

If, instead of potash, ammonia be added to the sulphate of copper, a similar blue precipitate will appear at first, but on adding a little more it will dissolve in the excess, and a splendid blue solution will result. The production of this blue colour with ammonia is an important test for the presence of a proto-salt of copper in any solution.

When a current of hydrogen is passed over protoxide of copper, heated to redness in a tube, in the same way as with sesquioxide of iron (v. page 60), water is produced, and a soft granular powder of metallic copper remains in the tube, which, however, does not, as in the case of iron, inflame in the air.

Salts of Protoxide of Copper.—Sulphate of Copper, $Cu\,O, S\,O_3$ (blue vitriol). This salt may be obtained by dissolving the protoxide in sulphuric acid. It forms large and beautiful blue crystals. These crystals contain five equivalents of water ($Cu\,O, S\,O_3 + 5\,H\,O$), which, however, may be expelled, and the salt obtained anhydrous, by the aid of heat. It is then an almost white powder, without crystalline form, which manifests a powerful affinity for water. This will be seen if some of the powder be placed in a little beaker, and about an equal bulk of cold water poured on it. The outside of the beaker will become sensibly warm.

Copper will dissolve in strong sulphuric acid with the aid of heat, a portion of the acid being decomposed to furnish the necessary oxygen to the copper, and sulphurous acid being consequently given off :—

$$Cu + 2\,(H\,O, S\,O_3) = Cu\,O, S\,O_3 + S\,O_2 + 2\,H\,O.$$

Nitrate of Copper, $Cu\,O, N\,O_5$, may be prepared by dissolving copper in nitric acid. Red fumes are given off, and a blue solution remains, from which crystals may be obtained on evaporation. These contain three equivalents of water, $Cu\,O, N\,O_5 + 3\,H\,O$, and are very soluble and deliquescent.

Metallic tin has a very curious action on this salt. Powder a little of it, and wrap it up with a drop or two of water in a small piece of tin-foil. The tin is so rapidly oxidized at the expense of the salt, that it sometimes catches fire.

The mineral called *malachite*, of which such beautiful ornaments are made, is a *carbonate of copper*. A somewhat similar carbonate, though containing a little more water, may be obtained by precipitating sulphate of copper with solution of carbonate of soda. The precipitate, at first blue, soon becomes green.

Other Compounds of Copper.—I have already referred to the *sulphide*. The *chloride* (Cu Cl) may be prepared by dissolving protoxide of copper in hydrochloric acid. It forms green crystals, and communicates a bright-green colour to flame (v. page 143).

Tests for Copper.—A piece of bright iron, such for instance as a knife-blade, becomes coated with the metal, when immersed in any solution containing copper.

Ferrocyanide of Potassium produces with proto-salts of copper a brown precipitate.

The *ammonia* test I have before alluded to.

Tungsten, W = 95.

This metal exists in considerable quantities in the mineral called *wolfram*, in combination with protoxide of iron. It is a white metal, is very brittle and very hard, and, next to platinum and gold, is the heaviest body known. The only interest which attaches to it, is from the fact which I have before mentioned, that its alloys with iron possess valuable properties.

SILVER, Ag = 108.

This beautiful and valuable metal has been from the most remote ages the object of admiration to men, and it is not surprising that such should have been the case, for it is frequently found native, and, when found, is readily worked, and not liable to rust or tarnish.

I have already mentioned the quantity which is extracted from English lead.

There are, besides, important mines of this metal in Chili, Mexico, and many other parts of the world.

When pure, silver is a white and brilliant metal, which is soft and easily cut, and rather heavier than copper. In a pure state it would be much too soft to be used for money, but this is rectified by alloying with it a little copper, which makes it harder. If you dissolve a silver coin—a fourpenny piece for instance—in nitric acid, you will notice that the solution has a pale-blue colour, and on adding excess of ammonia to it, this will change into the deep blue which I mentioned before as so characteristic of copper.

Protoxide of Silver, $Ag\,O$.—This, which is the only important oxide, may be prepared by adding excess of potash to a solution of nitrate of silver. It falls as a pale-brown precipitate.

Oxide of silver, when exposed to a red heat, parts with its oxygen, metallic silver being left behind.

Salts of Oxide of Silver.—By far the most important is the *nitrate*, $Ag\,O, N\,O_5$, which is obtained by dissolving the metal in nitric acid, and evaporating the solution down till it crystallizes.

Solution of nitrate of silver is of great importance to chemists as a test for chlorine, which it precipitates from all solutions which contain it (v. page 97).

Other Compounds of Silver.—Chloride of Silver, Ag Cl, is produced whenever a solution containing silver is mixed with a solution containing chlorine, or hydrochloric acid. It is quite insoluble in water, and even in nitric acid, but is readily dissolved by ammonia.

Chloride of silver, as well as some other compounds of silver, possesses the curious property of blackening, or rather turning purple, when exposed to light. It is on this property of the salts of silver, the reason of which is still somewhat uncertain, that the art of photography mainly depends. This art, which has now grown to such a wonderful extent and perfection, must be regarded as one of the most beautiful adaptations of chemistry to the wants and conveniences of every-day life, that has ever been afforded us. The *bromide* and *iodide* of silver are very similar to the chloride.

Platinum, Pt = 98·7.

This valuable metal is found, unfortunately, only in very small quantities. It is always met with native, in small grains associated with small proportions of still scarcer metals. It is white, and rather hard, is very malleable and ductile, being in this latter respect inferior only to iron. It is the heaviest body known. Platinum does not tarnish even at the highest temperature, and it can only be fused by the heat of the oxy-hydrogen blow-pipe. Deville has recently contrived a crucible made of lime (one of the few substances which resist the action of this intense heat), in which he has succeeded in fusing tolerably large quantities of the metal.

Platinum is insoluble in all acids. It will dissolve in chlorine water, but the usual solvent for it is what is called *nitro-hydrochloric acid*, or *aqua regia*. This is a mixture of one part of nitric acid with four parts of hydrochloric acid. Its intense solvent power depends upon the fact that free chlorine is present in it. When platinum is dissolved in this way, a yellow salt, the *bichloride of platinum*, $Pt\,Cl_2$, is produced.

Platinum is almost exclusively used for chemical purposes. It is such a bad conductor of heat, that one end of a very short piece of wire or foil (foil is thin sheet metal) may be heated to whiteness while the other is held in the hand. It is much to be regretted that platinum is not more abundant, for in many respects it is admirably adapted for culinary and other useful purposes. Supposing, for instance, it were possible to make ladles, spoons, and saucepans of it. Not only would they never rust or corrode, but when they became dirty they could be cleaned and made quite bright again by simply heating them red-hot in the fire.

Platinum may be obtained in a finely divided state by precipitation from the bichloride. In this state it is the black, soot-like powder, known as "spongy platinum," and has a very remarkable effect on certain gases. If a little of it be introduced into an explosive mixture of oxygen and hydrogen (v. page 55), the two gases immediately combine with explosion, and water is formed. If a piece of it be held in a current of hydrogen proceeding from a jet, the hydrogen will combine with the oxygen of the air rapidly, and enough heat will be evolved to make the platinum red-hot, and this in its turn will inflame the hydrogen. A lamp, named "Döbereiner's lamp," after its inventor, has been contrived on this principle, by which a light may be obtained by simply turning on a stop-cock. A jet of hydrogen is thus directed on the spongy platinum, and the effects I have just mentioned, follow. Of course a paper match or a taper may be kindled from the hydrogen.

This curious property is not confined to *spongy* platinum, as you may see by the following experiment:—

Take a common spirit-lamp, cut the wick rather short, and surround it with a coil of thin platinum wire about half an inch high, *a* fig. 45. Light the

Fig. 45.

lamp, and when the wire is red-hot blow it out again. The wire, instead of cooling immediately, will continue to glow as long as any spirit remains in the lamp, a peculiar smell being evolved during the time. In this experiment the vapour of the spirit is oxidized by the action of the platinum, and a number of volatile products are obtained. The supposed reason of this property of platinum is, that it has the power of condensing gases on its surface, and thus bringing their particles (for gases have particles, as well as solids and liquids) more closely in contact.

Gold, Au = 197.

From the remotest times this beautiful metal has been more highly valued than any other. It is the first which is mentioned in the Bible, and it appears to have been in all ages and in all countries, as it is with us, the standard by which the value of other things has been estimated, so that the word is very frequently used in a general sense to denote riches.

Gold is always found native. It occurs in small quantities in almost every part of the world. Even in our own country it may, by proper means, be separated from some of the older rocks.

I have seen ingots weighing three or four ounces, which have in this way been extracted from the crushed rock, but the quantity obtained is not sufficient to pay for the working.

The chief supply of gold is now obtained from California and Australia, although the metal was only discovered in those places a very short time ago.

Gold is a beautiful yellow metal, very soft, and very heavy. It is the most malleable and ductile of all metals known (v. page 133). It requires a white heat for fusion.

In a pure state, gold is far too soft to be used for coin. The metal of which our English sovereigns are made, is an alloy of gold with one-twelfth of its weight of copper.

Gold is quite insoluble in all acids, though it may, like platinum, be dissolved in aqua-regia.

The solution consists of *terchloride of gold*, $Au\ Cl_3$.

To illustrate this, take two glasses; pour a little hydrochloric acid into one, and a little nitric acid into the other. Put a piece of gold-leaf into each, and stir them; the gold will not dissolve. Now mix the two acids, with the gold in them. Red fumes will be given off, and the metal will be dissolved, yielding a yellow solution.

Gold exhibits a very weak affinity for oxygen, or, in fact, for any of the non-metallic elements. All its compounds with them are decomposed by heat, the metal being reduced to the metallic state.

INDEX.

	PAGE
Acid, Antimonic	166
„ Arsenic	162
„ Arsenious	162
„ Boracic	130
„ Carbonic	118
„ Chloric	92
„ Chromic	179
„ Hydrochloric	94
„ Hydrofluoric	99
„ Hydrosulphuric	103
„ Hypochlorous	92
„ Hyponitric	84
„ Manganic	178
„ Nitric	79
„ Nitro-Hydrochloric	188
„ Oxalic	117
„ Permanganic	178
„ Phosphoric	111
„ Silicic	130
„ Sulphuric	102
„ Sulphurous	101
Acid salts	138
Acids, Definition of	22
„ Hydrogen	95
„ Oxygen	83
„ Polybasic	136
Affinity	18
Air	75
Allotropy	44
Alloys	133
Alum	152
Alumina	151
„ Silicate of	152
Aluminum	151
Amalgams	134
Ammonia	86

	PAGE
Ammonium	87
Amorphous phosphorus	110
Analysis	54
Antimony	165
„ Terchloride of	166
„ Teroxide of	165
„ Tersulphide of	166
Aqua-fortis	79
Aqua-regia	188
Armstrong guns	134
Arsenic	162
Arseniuretted hydrogen	163
Balloons	50
Barium	147
„ Chloride of	147
Baryta	147
„ Nitrate of	147
„ Sulphate of	147
Bases, Definition of	23
Basic salts	138
Basins	8
Beakers	8
„ Manipulation with, &c.	155
Bee-hive shelf	31
Bell-metal	133
Bismuth	166
Black-lead	115
Bleaching	91
Blowpipe	125
„ Oxy-hydrogen	127
Borax	130
Boron	130
Bottles	5
Brass	133

	PAGE
Brimstone	100
Bromine	98
Calcium	148
„ Chloride of	149
Calomel	171
Carbon	115
„ Bisulphide of	129
Carbonic Oxide	116
Carburetted hydrogen	122
Charcoal	116
Chlorine	89
Chlorine water	91
Choke damp	127
Chromium	179
„ Sesquioxide of	179
Cinnabar	168
Clay	152
Coal	120
Coal-gas	120
Coal-tar	122
Cobalt	180
„ Chloride of	181
„ Nitrate of	181
„ Protoxide of	180
Coke	121
Combination different from Mixture	16
Combining proportions	62
Combustion	41
Condensation	71
Copper	182
„ Nitrate of	184
„ Oxides of	183
„ Sulphate of	184
Corks, Boring of	26
Corrosive Sublimate	171
Crucibles	8
Crystallization	69
„ Water of	73
Davy lamp	127
Decomposition, Double	21
Deflagrating spoon	37
Deliquescence	111
Delivery-tube	28
Dew	77
Diamond	115
Displacement, Collection by	49
Distillation	70
„ Destructive	121
Distilled water	8
Drying of flasks	7
Ductility	133
Dutch gold	91
Earths	151
Efflorescence	146
Elements	10
„ List of	15
Equivalent, Meaning of term	64
Ether, Solution of phosphorus in	109
Filtration	72
Fire	41
Fire damp	127
Flame, Nature of	123
Flames, Coloured	143
Flasks	6
Fluorine	98
Four Elements	10
Frost	77
Funnels	72
„ Thistle-headed	47
Fusible metal	167
Gas jar	30
Glass	131
Gold	190
„ Terchloride of	191
Graphite	115
Green fire	144
Gun-cotton	82
Gun-metal	133
Gunpowder	145
Haloid Salts	96
Halogen	95
Hydracids	95

	PAGE
Hydrates of Oxides . .	142
Hydraulic main . . .	122
Hydrogen	46
„ Binoxide of . .	73
Indigo turned yellow by Nitric acid . . .	82
Invisible Ink . . .	181
Iodine	97
Iron	172
„ Chlorides of . . .	175
„ Oxides of . . .	174
„ Sulphates of . . .	175
Jets	57
Kelp	97
Lamps	5
Laughing-gas . . .	78
Law of neutrality . .	137
Laws of combining proportion	62
Lead	153
„ Acetate of . . .	158
„ Carbonate of . .	158
„ Chromate of . .	180
„ Nitrate of . . .	158
„ Oxides of . . .	154
Lead paper	106
Lead tree	21
Lime	148
„ Carbonate of . .	149
„ Chloride of . .	92
„ Hydrate of . .	149
„ Sulphate of . . .	149
Lime light	127
Lime water	38
Litmus	22
Lucifer matches . . .	93
Magnesia	150
„ sulphate of . .	150
Magnesium	150
„ Chloride of .	150
Malachite	185

	PAGE
Manganese	176
„ Oxides of . .	176
„ Salts of . .	177
Manipulation with Beakers	155
Marsh gas	122
Marsh's Test for Arsenic .	163
Mauve	122
Mercury	168
„ Chlorides of . .	171
„ Nitrates of . .	171
„ Oxides of . .	170
„ Sulphide of . .	172
Metallic lustre . . .	132
Metals, Fusibility of . .	133
„ Weight of . . .	132
Mineral Chameleon . .	178
Mixture	16
Mosaic Gold . . .	161
Neutrality	135
„ Law of . .	137
Neutral salts	137
Nickel	182
„ Protoxide of . .	182
Nitre	145
Nitrogen	74
„ Binoxide of . .	84
„ Protoxide of . .	78
Olefiant gas	122
Orpiment	162
Oxides	43
Oxidizing agents . . .	85
„ flame . . .	126
Oxygen	25
Oxy-acids	83
Oxy-salts	85
Ozone	44
Pewter	134
Phosphoretted hydrogen .	113
Phosphorus	106
Platinum	187
„ Bichloride of .	188
„ Spongy . . .	188

	PAGE
Pneumatic trough	29
Potash	141
„ Bichromate of	180
„ Chlorate of	92
„ Manganate of	178
„ Nitrate of	145
Potassium	139
„ Chloride of	92
Precipitate	21
Quicksilver	168
Rain	77
Receiver	71
Red cabbage, Infusion of	24
Red fire	144
Red lead	159
Reducing flame	126
Respiration	42
Retort	71
„ stands	6
„ Tube	27
Salt, common	147
Salts	23
Saltpetre	145
Sand-bath	80
Selenium	114
Silicon	130
Silk, Action of Nitric Acid on	81
Silver	186
„ Chloride of	187
„ Nitrate of	186
„ Protoxide of	186
Smalt	181
Soaps	142
Soda	145
„ Carbonate of	146
„ Nitrate of	146
„ Phosphate of	146
„ Sulphate of	146
Soda-water	120
Sodium	145
Sodium, Chloride of	147
Solutions	68
Spirit-lamp	5
Starch, Iodide of	98
Steam	70
Stills	71
Strontia	148
„ Nitrate of	148
„ Sulphate of	148
Strontium	148
Sublimation	101
Sulphates	103
Sulphides	104
Sulphur	100
Supports	6
Symbols	66
Synthesis	54
Test tubes	7
Tin	159
„ Bisulphide of	161
„ Chlorides of	161
„ Oxides of	161
Tin-plate	160
Tubes, Cutting and bending of	25
Tungsten	185
Turpentine, Action of Nitric Acid on	81
Vermilion	172
Vitriol, Oil of	102
Wash-bottle	156
Water	53
Wire-gauze, Flames stopped by	128
Zinc	167
„ Chloride of	168
„ Oxide of	168
„ Sulphate of	168
Zinc, Granulated	46
Zones of flame	124

LONDON: PRINTED BY WILLIAM CLOWES AND SONS, STAMFORD STREET.

CPSIA information can be obtained
at www.ICGtesting.com
Printed in the USA
LVHW101356070722
722950LV00003B/41